Triangles: A Novella and Two Stories
by
Rolf Semprebon

UBU PRESS

This is a work of fiction. Any resemblances to persons alive or dead, or to actual events, are purely coincidental.

Triangles: A Novella and Two Stories
Published by Ubu Press, Portland, Oregon

ISBN (print paperback): 979-8-9988312-0-1

Library of Congress Control Number: 2025909107

Cover design: G. M. Donley

Printed in USA
First edition June 2025

Table of Contents

INTRODUCTION

The three stories within these pages do not have much in common, other than they all rely on multiple points of view (something I tend to do in my fiction, also known by the derogatory term "head hopping,") and they were mostly written during the first Trump administration, and are set in that turbulent time, or afterwards. This book is being published early in a new MAGA era that promises (threatens) to be even more turbulent.

I could have added one or two more stories, but with the short novel "Triangles" as the anchor story (not meant that as a pun since the work is set entirely on a yacht) a trio of stories made more sense. In the story "Triangles," Trump, and MAGA are not mentioned, merely hinted at when a character states that on the vessel: "no discussing politics, especially with how heated it's become." Political elements appear more in the second story, "Grave Incident" and dominate the final piece, "Q D'Etat," which might be described as a "political drama."

The germ for "Q D'Etat" came from an event called NaNoWriMo (National Novel Writing Month) where writers challenge themselves to write a 50,000 word novel during the month of November. I took up the challenge in 2020 with an idea of a novel set during the election that year and its aftermath, expecting violence and chaos I assumed would happen to give me interesting plot ideas. That attempt was a complete mess; I gave up halfway through the month with far less than 50,000 words, and the violence and chaos didn't happen until two months later, on January 6th. It's probably better, I think, to wait and have time to reflect when one writes about historic events. So the novel "Q D'Etat" abandoned, several months later I took the title and one scene (the hardware store with the Q sticker) and built a more focused plot and characters around it, and voila, the final story in this volume.

"Grave Incident" was an idea kicking around my head for years, the idea of a story where something tragic happens, but to tell it with the tragic event as the final scene, by alternating the events that lead up to that tragedy in chronological order and the aftermath in reverse chronology. The story pulling in from both the past and the future to that one fatal event. Nonlinear narrative has always fascinated me, and I liked the idea of the story closing in from both sides of time in a pincer move to reach the climatic event at the center. The story is much less a thriller than the other two, and more of a family drama, and maybe a mystery, in an unconventional sense, and mostly, is an experiment.

Then we have the title story, which is not quite long enough to be a novel, but longer than a novella. "Triangles" originally began as a radio theater script. From late 2002 to early 2018 I hosted a monthly radio theater show, The Ubu Hour, on KBOO community FM radio, writing scripts, along with production and editing. The radio theater version of "Triangles" ran on July 2016, and can be podcasted here: https://kboo.com/media/50945-triangles. Several years later, I decided to turn it into prose, with no idea if it would be a short story or a novel. The novella/novel has the same general events, but with some drastic changes, better developed characters (I hope, ha ha) and a more cohesive plot. Inspired by the movies Dead Calm and Triangle, it's a thriller and a horror story without paranormal or fantasy elements, taking place entirely within the confines of a yacht. Read at your own risk.

Thank you for reading. If you enjoy these stories, please tell your friends about this book, post a review on Amazon or Goodreads, or share on social media. And look for my upcoming novels, which Ubu Press hopes to publish soon.

ACKNOWLEDGMENTS

Though writing is a solitary act, this book would not have been possible without the help and encouragement of many people. My thanks to my critique groups, Portland Writers Workshop and The Critiquery, both of which had to endure earlier versions of one or more of these stories, and helped me refine my vision on it. Also thanks to KBOO FM, community radio station in Portland where an early radio theater version of "Triangles" aired. Thanks to encouragement from Willy Vlautin, Patricia Horvath, and G. M. Donley, who are all tremendous writers. Also thanks to the writers at the various Shut Up & Write and Write More sessions in Portland. And thanks to my mother and my brothers Jeff and Andrew, and other relatives. (And my father, who passed away about 10 years before I'm writing this.) And another thanks to Greg Donley for his design assistance.

I'm sure there's others I should be thanking, but I can't think of them now . . .

TRIANGLES

1: Beatrice

"I think he just pulled up," Kate Mayhew says, leaning over the rail on the main deck of the yacht.

"About time! Just like Charlie, to hold us up." Beatrice Welch follows Kate's gaze, past the other vessels to the marina parking lot, where a car pulls into a space.

"Only ten minutes late, Beatrice," James Welch, Beatrice's husband says, brushing a hand through his sandy hair. "Give him some slack."

"I've given him slack since he was born," Beatrice snaps back. "That's the problem. Everyone gives Charlie too much slack."

Neither her husband James nor her sister-in-law Kate knows Charlie the way she does. Thirteen years younger than her, Charlie was always the baby. As Beatrice listens to the sail above flap in the breeze, the thought comes to her head, a person is like a sail, too much slack, and a boat merely drifts. A taut sail moves the vessel; a person needs that same tautness, that same fullness, to not be adrift. Charlie has drifted aimlessly his whole forty years of life.

"Looks like he brought someone," Kate says.

Beatrice squints towards the car and the two shapes that climb out. "Is it Sally?"

"No. Not Sally," Kate replies.

Beatrice glances at Kate, who still has her eyes trained on the parking lot. Kate with her short bob of ruffled graying-brown hair and angular nose, and with her sharp eyes, Kate could almost be a bird, a hawk or eagle, as she stares across the distance at the parking lot. Cool, calm Kate.

"Not Sally," Kate repeats. "Someone new."

"A new woman?" Beatrice peers at the car and the blurred figures, wishing she had the binoculars with her. "But he didn't tell us."

"You know Charlie. Always unpredictable." Kate chuckles.

"He brings a stranger on board? What is he thinking?"

"It'll be fine," Kate says.

"No consideration for the rest of us. Stuck on this boat the whole day."

"Relax, Beatrice. She might be a stranger now, but we'll soon know her. You have James, and I have Alfie. It's good Charlie brought someone."

"I suppose." Beatrice groans. "It's the way Charlie springs this on us. Does this woman even know Dad?"

This is their final voyage on the *Trinity*, the fifty-five-foot custom yacht owned by the father of Beatrice, Charlie, and their older brother Alfie. It's also the first time the three siblings have been together since their father's funeral, three months earlier. They are sailing out of Anacortes to a hidden cove west of Port Angeles to scatter Farley Mayhew's ashes.

Charlie and the woman walk along the side of the lot towards the entrance to the docks.

"Charlie has a new girlfriend," Kate says. "No big deal."

"It's his choice in women that concerns me. Sally was okay, but the ones before her? Lock all the silver and anything else small and of value."

Kate laughs. "That girl before Sally wasn't too bad. Nothing to do about it now."

Beatrice sighs and thinks how Kate shrugs off the problem, pushes it under the carpet and hopes it goes away. And maybe Kate is right in this case. Nothing to be done. Make the best of Charlie's faux pas.

"James, did you know about this?" Beatrice turns to her husband.

James stares at the parking lot, his face stern. He mutters a word under his breath.

"James? You were with Charlie last Tuesday."

James turns to her. "No. He said nothing to me. Maybe she's some floozy he picked up two days ago."

"Even Charlie wouldn't . . ." Beatrice shakes her head.

A smile spreads across James' face. "Maybe we should untie the *Trinity* and leave without him? Can you imagine the look on Charlie's face, standing at the dock?"

The figures in the lot reach the entrance to the docks. The taller one, Charlie, and the smaller one, a slash of crimson, the woman. They hold hands as they walk towards the yacht. The woman wears a red skirt and blouse. Charlie has a grin and a relaxed stroll, though they are late.

James clears his throat. "I'll help Alfie lower the sails to leave the dock." He starts to move past Beatrice.

"I can do that," Blocking his way, Kate steps to the ladder up the side deck that leads to the bow.

"You don't have to, Kate. Why not relax here with Beatrice?" James flourishes his hand towards the lounge chairs at the center of the main deck.

"I like doing the sails with Alfie." Kate raps her hand on the bulwark. "Last time with this old girl. I'll miss her."

"Kate is right. You stay here, James," Beatrice says. James has his back to her as he looks towards Kate. Kate turns her back and starts up the ladder, and James seems to take a second too long before he turns to Beatrice. Was he checking out Kate's ass? Beatrice wonders for a moment, Kate who has managed to keep slim at age forty-four, eight years younger than Beatrice.

James smiles. "What do you expect from your brother Charlie?"

"A bit of consideration for Dad," Beatrice replies. "Not visiting the hospital before he good-byed."

Charlie and the woman are closer now. He has a large duffelbag on his shoulder and the woman a day pack. Charlie waves. The woman is younger than Charlie, wavy black hair fans her big eyes and pixie face. The red cotton skirt is above her knees.

"She looks bohemian," Beatrice says.

A frown weighs on James' lips and his eyes narrow. "Let's make the best of the situation. I don't like it any more than you. We're here for your father, not that punk and whatever piece he's dragging aboard. Just ignore Charlie and his . . ."

"As if that's easy, stuck on this yacht for the day." She quietly says this because Charlie is within earshot as he reaches the gangway.

Charlie lets go of the woman's hand and starts up the ramp. "Finally got here!" The woman follows him, her face dumbstruck as she takes in the *Trinity*. Best to make the best of it, Beatrice thinks regretfully.

2: James

Suppressing his anger, James Welch watches Charlie and Evie board the vessel.

"You're late, Charlie!" Beatrice snips. "We were ready an hour ago."

James does not correct his wife; Alfie had only minutes earlier finished preparing the vessel to launch.

Charlie ignores Beatrice's remark. "Beatrice. James. This is Evie," he gushes. A knot clenches at James's bowels as he makes his best effort not to glare at Charlie. "Evie, my sister Beatrice, and her husband James." Charlie does a slight bow, always the court jester.

"Nice meeting you both," Evie says. James murmurs a hello. He observes her at the edge of his vision, and she also avoids eye contact. Her gaze is wide as she stares up the mast.

"Nice meeting you, Evie." Beatrice chirps vacuously. "Charlie tells us so little what he's up to."

"It's . . . huge!" Evie says. "I thought it would be a small boat."

"It won't seem so big after you've been on it for seven hours," Beatrice quips sourly.

"This is Evie's first time at sea," Charlie says. "Go easy on her."

I'll go real easy on you, James thinks.

"Not true," Evie pipes up. "I was on a ferry once."

"A ferry?" Beatrice says.

"First time on a sailing yacht," Charlie corrects himself.

"So Evie, what do you do for a living?" Beatrice asks.

"Evie's a freelance writer," Charlie says.

"I'm also a server," Evie adds.

"A server? A legal assistant who serves papers to people?"

"For fucks sake, Beatrice, don't be stupid," James mutters to himself.

"No, Beatrice. She works at a restaurant." Charlie smirks as if he's proud of this.

"Just part-time," Evie adds.

"A waitress." Beatrice's tone is withering. "I suppose that's where you met Charlie?"

"It's just part-time until she makes more from writing," Charlie says.

"So what kind of things do you write?" Beatrice asks.

"I'm working on a novel." Evie hefts the bag to the other shoulder. "A deconstruction of Moby Dick."

"We'll talk later," Charlie says. "Need to bring our stuff below. And I want to show Evie the *Trinity*." With their bags, Charlie and Evie head towards the hatch that leads down to the cabin.

"So what do you think, James?" Beatrice asks.

"A ferry? Who hasn't ridden a ferry?" James forces a grin on his lips.

"That's not what I meant."

"What did you mean?" he asks.

"About the girl. What do you think of her?"

He shrugs for an answer.

"Do you find her pretty?"

"No," he says, but his voice sounds hollow in his head. "Not to me at least. She looks like something from the back of classified in the weekly freebies when they still ran those ads."

"Stop joking, James. What would father think?"

He'd probably want to jump her bones, James tells himself. Beatrice's father was known as frisky-fingers Farley because of his inappropriate behavior around women half his age or younger, not that James could besmirch big daddy in front of Beatrice. "She's low class, but that's where Charlie dwells, the gutter."

"I guess we'll wait and see." Beatrice stares out at the dock.

"It'll be fine, dear," he replies, to calm her down. "Make the best of it." James gives Beatrice a hug. "Take your meds if it makes you nervous."

"No. I want this to be like the funeral." Beatrice takes a deep breath. "I might take one right before we scatter father's ashes and by the time we are done it'll kick in to ease the trip home, but not before."

James doesn't want to press the point, but at least he knows the pills are in the side pocket of her carry-on in the cabin. He can't go down to the cabin, or she will think he's doing it to ogle Evie, or to try to catch her changing clothes in the berth.

No big deal, James thinks. The meds are her security blanket the way her older brother Alfie always carries a gun. Like the day of the funeral, she would be fine not taking one until late, but Charlie introduces an extra element, Evie, to disturb the calm.

James is furious at Charlie and yet powerless to do anything about it as he gazes at his wife and hopes she doesn't suspect anything. With Evie aboard, James will feel obligated to stay near Beatrice so as not to arouse her suspicion, instead of hanging out with Charlie to get drunk, to make the day with his in-laws and his wife more tolerable.

Alfie appears from the side deck, having lowered the sails after raising them to inspect them. "Cast off!"

James pulls up the gangway and leans over to untie the line from the large rusted cleat in the weathered dock. Alfie, a few years older than Beatrice and fifteen years older than Charlie, steps past them to reach the wheel, at the back of the craft. The helm console is set on a wide platform, the quarterdeck, several feet above the main deck at the stern. At the captain's chair behind the wheel, Alfie turns on the engine and begins to steer. The *Trinity* glides past the other yachts. Once out of the marina, Alfie will turn off the motor, raise the sails back up, and set them to the wind.

"Hey, Captain!" James calls out over the flapping of the sails and the drone of the engine. "How are we looking for weather?"

"Looking for what?" Alfie calls back, looking over the steering console.

James steps closer. "How does it look? The weather?"

"North wind, so it'll be easy sailing to the cove," Alfie yells back. "Warm weather and sunshine. Couldn't ask for better. Dad would have loved it. I wish we could stay out a couple days, catch fish.”

“Too bad you sold the fishing gear, Alfie.”

“Not all. One harpoon gun left. In case we see a big one.”

James gives him a thumbs-up and strolls back to Beatrice. “You hear that? Nice weather all day.”

Beatrice nods. “That’s good.”

The marina and the city of Anacortes fall quickly behind them. Soon they will be out of sight of land in the vast empty sea. James pats his wife on the shoulder. “This will be a nice voyage.”

In his gut he’s not so sure.

3: Evie

Down into the bowels of the vessel, the room is inlaid with mahogany and brass. Evie Lavie is spellbound as she glances around. “What’s that?” She points to to a colorful urn, wedged against the wall by a toolbox.

Charlie Mayhew looks over from the kitchenette. “That’s my father.”

“Your father?” Confused Evie steps closer. The urn is a foot tall and half that wide, a portrait in a triangle on its shiny black surface. The man’s face, a black and white image, glowers out of the frame. Beneath the picture is a name in gold cursive: Farley Mayhew.

“Farley? That’s you dad?”

“Uh-huh. His ashes.”

“What? No!” She backs away from the urn. “You’re kidding, right?”

“No.” He puts his arms around hers.

“Why is it on the ship?”

“They want to scatter his ashes in the cove. The whole purpose of the trip.”

“Charlie!” Evie pushes his arm off. “Why didn’t you tell me?”

Charlie shrugs. “Didn’t think it was important.”

“Not important?”

“No. I want you to see the cove where we used to go. The beach, you can only reached it by sea. This is our only chance.”

“You should have mentioned . . . I thought this would be . . .” She lets the sentence hang. She thought it would be a leisure cruise, not a ritual for the recently deceased. If she had known, would she be here? She’s not sure. She’s upset Charlie didn’t tell her, but she suppresses it to avoid conflict. After all, she did want to experience a ride on a yacht. Research for her novel.

"You wait and see," Charlie says. "The cove is beautiful. We'll have a good time. Sorry for not mentioning the dad thing. I try not to think about him too much."

"Charlie, you're lucky you had a father."

"Don't know about that. Not my father." He walks to the kitchenette, tucked in one corner of the interior room of the ship.

How odd, Evie wishes for a father she never knew, and he wishes he didn't have one. Maybe he only thinks that, coping with the recent death. Evie notices a change has come over him, his casual cheerfulness dampened, but she can not pinpoint if it's from when they got on the boat, or a moment ago, at the sight of his father's urn.

Evie walks over to the kitchenette. Charlie unzips the duffelbag on the dinette table and paws through it.

"Should I be here?" she asks.

"What do you mean?"

"Maybe I should've waited to meet your family." She has her hands curled in front of her as she steps to the table.

"Nonsense." He pulls out the fifth of Johnny Walker Blue and places it on the table next to the fifth of Balvenie triple cask 16 single malt. He looks up at her with a smile. "I couldn't decide which to bring. But I think we'll start with the Walker."

So he brought both expensive bottles of whiskey, though back at the condo he told her he meant to bring one. "Don't change the subject, Charlie. Do you think I should get off the boat?"

"Yacht," he corrects her, putting an arm around her shoulder. "Besides, too late to get off. We've left the dock."

She pulls out of his grip and looks out the small round window. The dock drifts away at an angle from the shore. She notices the hum of the engine, and that the floor beneath them undulates more quickly, the arrhythmic creaking of the cabin more pronounced, as the yacht attacks the waves and leaves the marina behind.

She should feel elated. On the drive up from Seattle she was excited, who wouldn't be at a chance to ride in a sailing yacht? When they first got out of the car and he pointed out the vessel, his enthusiasm mirrored hers. The sails, two large pastel purple triangles, leashed to the mast like large restrained raptors. Below the sails, the vessel itself, the *Trinity*, was larger than she imagined in her head, like a small ship.

But once aboard, she was unsettled by the cold looks she got from Charlie's smug brother-in-law and his sister Beatrice, a heavy-set middle-aged woman with an imperious stare. And Charlie not telling her the trip is to spread the patriarch's ashes . . . The excitement of the yacht had quelled her nervousness meeting Charlie's family, but now it came back to her. "I don't think they want me here. James and your sister."

Charlie shrugs. "Beatrice always acts that way at first."

"And James? Wouldn't even look at me. Like we never met."

"That's how he wants it like I told you in the car. Never told Beatrice about that other night we went out drinking."

"I hope he doesn't get too drunk again," she says.

"Who cares about them? I want you here." Charlie pulls her into his arms and kisses her on the lips.

"I want them to like me, Charlie," Evie murmurs into his ear while he kisses her neck. "They're your family."

"Don't worry about it."

"Do you love me?"

"Of course I do." He holds her tighter in his arms. "More than anything, Evie."

"Even though I'm not . . . like them?"

"What do you mean?" Charlie pulls out a flask and fills it with Johnny Walker.

"With their boats and fancy cars and nice clothes and hoity-toity airs."

"Who cares about them. They're all crazy anyway. And they'll accept you once they know you."

A door at the far end of the space creaks open. Evie and Charlie turn towards the sound. A woman comes down the ladder steps from the front end of the boat. She reaches the bottom of the steps. When she turns, Evie is jolted by recognition. She knows Kate. What a coincidence! She smiles at Kate, but Kate has her eyes on Charlie.

"Charlie, hope I wasn't interrupting."

"Not really," he says. "We're about to do a shot and head back up. Kate, this is my girlfriend, Evie."

"Kate?"

"Hi, Evie," Kate steps towards them. "You here to help see off dear old Farley?"

"You two know each other?" Charlie asks, puzzled.

4: Charlie

Charlie notices as soon as Kate enters the cabin. The surprise on Evie's face, the look Kate gives Evie. They have met before; he guesses it aloud.

Kate nods and approaches.

"We have met before, haven't we?" Kate says to Evie. "What was it, two years ago?"

"Yes. In Portland."

"That's right. Why don't you pour me a shot too, Charlie?"

"I'll get another glass." Charlie walks over to the cabinets. Kate and Evie whisper to each other, barely audible over the creaks of the yacht. What is Kate saying to her? Something about him? He almost catches one word, "nothing," or "loving." Kate, next to Evie, smiles at him as he comes back with the third glass.

"So you met in Portland?" he asks.

"You didn't bring any . . .?" Kate puts her thumb and forefinger together and brings them to her lips.

"Of course we did," Charlie laughs. "I'll roll a couple of bombers before we go above. So how do you know each other?"

"We met briefly at a cafe," Kate says. "We had a nice talk."

"That's it?" Charlie pours the three shots.

"Pretty much. She's quite a catch, Charlie." Kate smiles.

Charlie smiles and shrugs, at a loss for words. Not only does Kate approve of Evie, but they already know each other, however briefly. Kate's acceptance means more to him than anyone else in the family, and if Kate gets along with Evie, his brother Alfie will too. What luck, Charlie rejoices, after Evie's fear of not fitting in. If everyone else comes around, Beatrice will have to join them.

Charlie hands a shot glass to each woman and picks the third off the table. "Bottoms up."

"Bottoms up," Kate and Evie echo in unison.

"The stuff is good," Charlie says. "Worth every penny."

Kate nods with approval as she places her shot glass down. "Listen, Charlie. Did you tell Evie . . .?" She points.

Charlie follows her finger to the bottle, a moment of confusion before it comes to him. "No, not yet."

"What is it, Charlie?" Evie asks.

"Two rules. No discussing politics, especially with how heated it's become, and keep the booze and drinking out of sight from Alfie," Charlie stashes the bottles back in his duffel bag. "Alfie doesn't approve. Ever since he went on that bender two years ago."

"It's not that he doesn't approve. He doesn't want the temptation," Kate corrects him. Then, to Evie. "Have you met my husband yet?"

"No," Evie replies. "Just Charlie's sister and James."

"Why don't I take you above deck to meet him while Charlie rolls those joints."

"I guess so." Evie glances at Charlie.

"You guys go up and I'll be there in five minutes." Charlie watches them take the steps to the main deck. He considers another shot, and thinks better of it, before he places the duffel bag next to the wall of the head, near the bow of vessel, and stashes the flask in the large front pocket of his shorts. He puts away the shot glasses and sits down at the table with papers and premium-grade cannabis.

Evie met Kate at a cafe in Portland. Two years ago? He wants to know more. Kate stayed in Portland several days when Alfie went on his bender. And Evie, that story she told him about Portland . . .

Footsteps pound down the steps. Charlie glances up. James storms towards him.

"The fuck, Charlie! What were you thinking?"

"What do you mean?" Charlie seals the joint and stands.

"Cut the shit. You know what I mean."

"Calm down, James. You want a shot?" Charlie pulls out the flask. "Johnny Blue."

"How could you be so . . ." James stops himself as if he realizes how much he's raised his voice. He starts again, voice at a normal level, but still burning with anger. "How can you be so stupid?"

"What's your problem? I told her not to mention the other night, James."

"Fuck you, Charlie. You know the problem. Why's she here?"

"Why not?" Charlie takes out the shot glasses and walks back over to put them on the table in the kitchenette.

"You shouldn't've brought her," James mutters.

"Who the hell're you to tell me who to bring?"

"Why're you creating problems, Charlie?"

"Fuck you, James. You told me you had a good time Tuesday night. You said you wanted to hang out with her again."

"Not here! Not stuck on this tub for the next seven hours. Not with Beatrice around. She didn't even take her meds this morning. Why didn't you bring Sally?"

Charlie shakes his head. "Sally is over. Ancient history."

"And this one? Evie? She never even met your dad."

"I love her, James. More than anyone."

"You can't be serious." James grabs the glass and takes a swig, emptying it.

Charlie has never seen James so angry, and the drink merely dulls the edge of that anger to leave it to seethe underneath. Face tightened in a scowl, James glares through hooded eyes and smacks the glass down hard.

"Sure I can. I am serious, James. Though the rest of you treat me like a joke.".

"This is no joke. You should think about the people around you, the family, instead of whatever new floozy you're fucking. You know how Beatrice has been, ever since your father died. And this was meant to be a family thing, for your dad. What would Farley think?"

Through clenched lips, Charlie replies. "He's dead. Who cares what he would think? I don't see why you're upset. After the fun we had the other night."

Why should James be angry? When he joined Charlie and Evie for dinner five days ago, they had fun. Beatrice was out of town for the night on a church social, so Charlie figured it would be a nice gesture, and Evie wanted to meet the family. The three of them got drunk and went back to Charlie's place to play a couple of hands of Rummy Tiles and drink more beers. Yet James didn't want his wife, Charlie's sister, to know Evie was there. Called Charlie the next day and made him promise if it came up in conversation, he and Charlie were alone that night. Beatrice and her jealous nature. What did she expect, Charlie thinks, marrying a man seven years younger than her? And a joker like James at that.

James narrows his eyes. "I suppose there's nothing we can do now." He reaches for the bottle again but stops. Charlie hears the footsteps. His sister Beatrice descends the steps into the cabin.

5: Beatrice

"Don't worry," James tells Beatrice at the edge of the main deck several minutes earlier. "We can't let an idiot like Charlie ruin the trip."

"Charlie is not an idiot," she replies. "Just inconsiderate." She glances over to see Kate emerge from the cabin, followed by Evie. Engaged in animated conversation too far away to make out words, they don't notice Beatrice and James at the rail corner as they head towards the rear. Kate, of course, the perfect hostess, Beatrice thinks to herself, while Evie peers around in awe.

Kate and Evie climb up to the steering console. Beatrice drifts closer, wondering what on earth Kate would say to the girl, but their words are drowned by the luffing of the sail.

Beatrice looks around. James is no longer on the main deck. She walks over to the open hatchway down to the cabin. She's about to call down to him when she hears his angry voice from below. She cannot make out his words, but he must be giving Charlie a much-deserved dressing down for inviting a stranger on the yacht. For once James isn't avoiding confrontation, when usually he leaves it to her to chastise Charlie's bad behavior. Perhaps Charlie will listen to James, whereas Charlie has ignored her advice for years, even decades.

She hurries down the companionway steps to lend James support. Charlie is seated at the dinette table, his back to her, and James stands at the far side. Charlie twists around to greet her. "Hi, Beatrice. You want a drink?" He indicates the bottle.

She shakes her head. "Maybe later. This isn't a party."

"No worries about that." Charlie screws on the cap tightly and places the bottle back in his bag.

"And don't drink too much," Beatrice says. "Being drunk out at sea is dangerous. People fall overboard and drown."

"Don't worry, dear," James says. "I'll make sure Charlie doesn't get drunk."

"We're just having one drink, Beatrice," Charlie adds. "For christsakes, have one to loosen up."

"Maybe later. It's not proper to drink in the morning."

James walks up to her and clutches her shoulders in his arms. "I told Charlie how we felt, how this is imposing on all of us."

"He should know. Nice for once to not have to be the one to tell him," she says.

"I'll talk to him more. No sense you being down here, like we're ganging up on him." James pulls her back towards the steps. "You should go above deck and see if Alfie needs help."

"I'm sure Alfie doesn't need help, and if he did, he'd send Kate down to get us."

"I'll head up soon." James jerks a thumb at Charlie. "I need to talk to Charlie more."

"Fine," Beatrice says. She starts up the steps, annoyed James doesn't want her there. Another of those guy things. She emerges on the main deck. The sun's warmth and the breeze caress her face and arms. She walks towards the lounge chairs in the center of the large deck.

Kate climbs down from the helm console in the rear and heads towards her.

"There's something in the water," Kate points starboard fifteen degrees from the bow.

"What is it?" Beatrice follows Kate's finger out the expanse of water but barely sees anything.

"Don't know. I'm getting the binoculars." Kate continues towards the cabin and vanishes down the hatch. Beatrice thinks about following her, but instead, she steps closer to the helm, around to the side where she sees Alfie, showing Evie how to steer the yacht.

6: Alfie

As he steers the *Trinity*, Alfred watches Kate and the other woman emerge from the cabin. They cross the main deck towards him. He slips the loop of line around one of the handles to hold the steering wheel in place and turns to greet them as they climb onto the helms deck with the steering console.

"Alfie, this is Evie, the friend Charlie brought," Kate says. "Evie, my husband, Alfred, but everyone calls him Alfie. Or Captain, when we're aboard."

"Nice meeting you, Captain," Evie says.

"Pleasure is mine," he replies, taking a long glance at her. "Welcome aboard the *Trinity*." Charlie had gushed about this woman the day before over the phone, and Alfred sees why. She is young and attractive, more attractive than Charlie's previous flings, even more attractive than Kate, Alfred thinks, with a tinge of envy for his younger brother. Charlie would have to bring her on board to show her off to the rest of the family, his trophy girlfriend.

"The *Trinity* is fifty-four-feet-nine-inches long. Custom built in the late 1940s." Alfie says.

The woman's eyes light up. "The wheel. It looks like the ones on a private ship."

"A private ship?" Alfred asks, tilting his head sideways to hear her better.

"A pirate ship."

"Never been on a pirate ship so I wouldn't know," Alfred tells her. "But this wheel, Dad wanted vintage, like what our ancestors would have used."

"Evie's never been on a yacht," Kate says.

"Really?" he says. "Let me show you the works. This button turns on the engine when the sails aren't used. And the throttle is here, to start the engine you have to do both." He starts up the engine to show her and then shuts it down again. "You want to steer?"

"Drive the boat?" She looks from him to Kate. "Are you guys kidding?"

"It's not like you'll crash into anything out here," Kate says.

"That's true," Evie replies. "Nothing but empty ocean. Just gray sea and blue sky. Like a minimalist painting."

"Come on. Over here by the wheel." Kate places a hand on Evie's back between her shoulders and gently pushes her to a large padded chair in front of the wheel. "Now put your hands on the handles, those wooden things coming out of the wheel. Like you are driving a car."

Evie sits at the edge of the seat. Alfred steps next to the wheel console, and reaches past her arm to grab one of the handles. With his other hand he lets off one the lines from the handle, and then the other. "Now, you keep it steady, make sure the needle stays on that red mark." He indicates the compass built into a small shelf on the console.

"You need a rest from the ship.. steering.." Evie says, her quiet voice half lost in the breeze.

"No. I don't need a rest," Alfred says. "Maybe later I'll let the others helm."

"She said you can see the rest of the yacht from here," Kate says.

"Yes," he nods. "You can see everything that happens on deck."

"Keep an eye on everyone because you're the captain," Evie says, gazing up at him with a sly smile.

Alfred takes a deep breath of the sea air, letting it fill his lungs and swell his chest with its salty vibrancy. Because you're the captain. With their father's death, it fell upon him to lead the family, and it weighs on him. He feels sadness every time his father's death comes into his head and a sense of disbelief that he'll never talk to his father again. Once Farley's ashes are scattered at Scalene Cove, the site of happy memories, and one of his father's favorite places, perhaps it will become easier.

Alfred feels guilty as he admits to his father's failed captaincy of the family. Both Alfred's brother and sister are crazy and irresponsible in their own way, because of the father's ineptitude as a father. Farley's inability to stick with one woman, his drinking, the failed business ventures, a decade separation from their mother, but now Farley Mayhew is gone. Alfred is still weak from the shock, but Alfred must now lead the family, set it on the right course, the way he has the *Trinity*, setting course southwest out of the Rosario Strait and west into the Strait of Juan de Fuca (pronounced "Want-a Fuck-a" by his father jokingly) past Port Angeles to the hidden Scalene Cove. He knows this trip like the back of his hand, and the dangers it once threatened are shadows from familiarity, though one can never fully trust the sea.

"Something's out there," Kate says. "Starboard, two o'clock." She points over the rail. "You see it, Evie?"

Evie squints, looking where Kate is pointing. "Yes! I do! Dark shape over there," and she points to it too. "You see it, captain?"

Alfred doesn't reply as he looks out at the ocean, starboard ahead of them. His eyes aren't what they used to be, and he refuses to wear glasses. He can barely make out the details of the front end of the yacht.

Kate comes up behind Evie at the wheel and turns the bezel ring on the compass several clicks. "Keep it there, Alfie," she says. He leans over Evie's arm on the wheel to glance down at the marker, thirteen-degree variation, and he pulls on the wheel to make the change in direction.

"What is it?" Evie asks.

"I don't know. I'll get the binoculars." Kate starts down the steps.

Alfred waits for Evie to follow her, so that he can get back behind the wheel, but Evie remains. Alone with the woman, Alfred feels awkward. He stands five feet away, watching her in profile as she continues to steer the yacht. She looks almost as young as his daughter, he thinks, though Charlie said she was thirty-four. Alfie looks at her face, and then his eyes travel down her neck to her cleavage, the blouse open at the top button, and from his position standing above her, the swell of her breasts is visible. What he would give to be young again.

She catches him looking down her shirt. "Do you wanna, sir?" she asks, as she twists towards him.

"Do I want to what?" Aflred chokes, feeling a heat in his belly.

"Steer the boat?" she says.

"Yes, that would be good." Get both hands back on the wheel, where they can't wander to places they shouldn't be. Back behind the wheel where he is in control. He holds the wheel while she slides out of the seat, and he sits down. She leans against the console, staring at the object Kate spotted out at sea, her rear end within reach of his hand if he leans out of the seat, the breezes fluttering the hem of her skirt against her slim thighs.

Once again he wishes he was young. He realizes he will soon have to take a piss. One of the agonies of middle age, a weak bladder. At least Beatrice is approaching so that she can take over the wheel.

Evie has her eyes glued to the object. "It feels so . . . wild. Lovely, beautiful sea," she says with a nervous laugh.

7: Evie

It's like going back in time, Evie thinks to herself as she stands at the railing while the sails push the vessel towards the thing Kate spotted, with the seagulls flying around it.

All around them the sea, primeval depths where all life once began, the eternal, endless sea . . . While on land mountains rise and fall, rivers erode canyons, and glaciers mold valleys, the sea was timeless, patient, never-changing.

She doesn't even have her cell phone on her. Charlie told her they'd have no service once they set sail, so the cell phone is in her backpack in the cabin below. They could be in an earlier century, as she thinks about the Pequod, the Hispaniola, the HMS Bounty, the Covenant, pirate ships and Spanish Galleons.

Alfie, Charlie's older brother, sits at the wheel a few feet away, wearing Bermuda shorts and a silk Hawaiian shirt unbuttoned to reveal the white hairs of his chest. She can see the resemblance, the same deep-set eyes, but Alfie is older by fifteen years, heavy-set, with varicose veins and a bald head. Is this what Charlie will look like at fifty-five? At least he's friendlier than Charlie's sister, but a bit crusty and humorless, as if something heavy weighed on him.

Evie hopes Kate gets back soon. She's nervous, to be on the deck alone with Alfie, not knowing what to say to him. But she wants to know Charlie's family, wants to be a part of it and get Charlie to be closer to them too. She needs to break free of her shyness with strangers. It wasn't there a minute ago when Kate was with them.

The sea inspires her. The infinite permutations that play out on its surface, the mysteriousness of its untamed depths. She wants to write something about it. To think one day in the future as the ice caps melt the sea will conquer more and more land.

She turns to Alfie. "It's so beautiful out here, don't you think?"

"Huh?" he turns towards her.

"The sea. It feels so wild. The lovely beautiful sea." She giggles at her attempt at poetry. He shrugs.

8: Beatrice

"Me. I feel so . . . wild. Let you do things to me." Spoken with a seductive giggle. Though Beatrice barely makes out the woman's words, their impact hits her. The brazen hussy. Up there on the steering console with Alfie, flaunting herself in front of him, laughing and wiggling her tight little buns in his face. And she says something like that. I'll let you do things to me. Offering herself up to Alfie, like a drug-crazed wanton nympho.

I knew it! Beatrice shudders, both angry and exhilarated her suspicions proven correct. In several quick steps, she reaches the base of the steering console, and looks up at them. From her vantage, she sees Eve's black lace panties beneath the cheap cotton skirt.

She climbs up to join them. "Hope I'm not interrupting."

"Beatrice, take over the helm for a moment." Alfie gets out of the seat. Evie looks out at the water, avoiding Beatrice.

"Sure, Captain." Beatrice grabs the wheel. Alfie steps away and she slides into the seat. "Maybe you should look for Kate, Alfie."

"Huh?" Alfie bends his head sideways to her.

"Never mind." She points below. Kate emerges from the cabin with the binoculars and moves quickly across the main deck. Alfie descends the steps, and a moment later they cross paths, a brief flurry of words, and Kate continues to the helm deck while Alfie heads to the cabin.

Beatrice is burning with the need to tell Kate what she witnessed, but to her chagrin, Evie doesn't leave. To make things worse, Kate ignores her, but instead joins Evie. They are seven feet away, at the rail, their backs to Beatrice, so close their shoulders and hips might be touching, as they look out at the ocean. Their words bubble into her ears, chirpy and cheerful at first, in a way she finds irritating.

"Do you see it, Kate?"

"Oh, dear, Evie. Not good."

"What is it, Kate?"

Kate murmurs something unintelligible and groans.

"Can I see?"

"Here, Evie. You focus by turning this."

"Yes." Evie squeals.

"Over there! Do you see it!"

"No . . . Yes! Kate! Whoa! That's awful . . . but I can't stop looking."

By now Beatrice makes out the object in the sea, a dark, shiny shape, and a dozen seagulls swarm around it, in the distance looking like flies. She secures the wheel and joins them.

Evie lowers the binoculars to look at Kate, her face ashen.

"Let me see." Beatrice grabs the binoculars out of Evie's hands. "And you shouldn't use those unless you put the strap around your neck."

Beatrice tracks across the waves until she sees it. The gulls, and below, a floating fusion of plastic and other debris, and what looks like some large fish trapped in it. The gulls dive down and rip more bloody pieces out of it, a dolphin or a porpoise, stuck in a floating isle of plastic flotsam. The belly of the creature is ripped open, and she even thinks she can see a baby falling half out of the stomach, being ripped apart by the beaks of the unrelenting birds, or maybe it's some spilled guts.

She lowers the binoculars and notices Evie is on the deck below, headed towards the cabins.

"Never seen anything like that," Kate says. "Horrible."

"I think it's a sign."

"A sign? That we're polluting the earth? Can't keep up with our trash?"

"More of an omen."

"What do you mean, Beatrice?" Kate asks.

Kate is too blind to see. Beatrice steps up to Kate and lowers her voice. "Kate?"

"What is it?"

"Can I be frank with you?"

"Of course." Kate turns from the ocean to face her. "What is it?"

Beatrice takes a deep breath. "I don't know how to tell you this."

"Tell me what?"

"Alfie."

"What about Alfie?"

"He's not as sharp as he once was," Beatrice says.

"That's his hearing," Kate says. "What are you saying?"

"Ever since Dad died, he hasn't been the same."

"He's upset but he'll get over it."

"I don't want to cast aspersions," Beatrice says, though that's exactly what she's doing. "But when Alfie was up here with that.." She glances around to make sure Evie hasn't returned to the deck and lowers her voice conspiratorially. ". . . that woman."

"What woman?"

"Charlie's . . ."

"Her name is Evie. What about her?" Kate asks.

"When Alfie was up here alone with her . . ."

"Come on, Beatrice. Are you telling me Alfie was putting moves on Evie?" Kate looks incredulous and amused.

"No. She was putting moves on him."

"Nonsense, Beatrice. Why would she do that? He's twenty years older than her."

"Have some common sense, Kate. She can probably see that Alfie has more money than Charlie. That Alfie pulls the strings on the estate."

"You're being ridiculous, Beatrice," Kate says. "Besides, if she was, Alfie wouldn't fall for it. I've talked to her a bit just now and she's quite charming."

"I suppose you're right. You did seem to get along nicely with her." Beatrice says.

"We all need to get along for the next seven hours."

"I guess so," Beatrice mutters. At least she's made Kate aware. Beatrice glances over to see the object, closer now, the details not quite visible to the naked eye, which makes it worse because her mind remembers an image far more gruesome and bloody.

That dying thing out there is an omen. Beatrice feels it in her soul. She's worried about Alfie. Her older brother has been un-moored, not himself, since their father died, and earlier. Weaker with every blow, the bad drinking jag two years ago, when Kate almost left him. He seemed to be recovering, but his father's death hit him as hard.

A gunshot, from the deck below, jerks Beatrice from her thoughts. It is quickly followed by another.

9: Alfie

". . . how stupid this is. If he found out . . ."

Alfred steps down into the cabin quickly, in time to see Charlie hide a bottle beneath the table, while James stops talking, and cranes his head around to see who has entered. "Hi, Alfie."

"You guys breaking out the booze early?" Alfred chides as he heads towards the head. "Not even noon." Before he reaches it, he begins unzipping his fly, as his bladder's plea for relief becomes a scream.

"Just one shot," James says. "Sorry about this."

"Sorry? You don't have to hide it from me." Alfred steps into the closet-sized chamber and lifts up the seat. As he pulls out his penis, he continues to talk to Charlie and James. "Kate has some funny ideas, but it's not like I don't know you two get tipsy on these cruises. Nothing escapes me aboard the *Trinity*."

Despite the agony in his gut, it takes a few seconds before he can urinate. A feeble stream pitters into the steel bowl. He is aware that James and Charlie, in the room outside, have stopped talking, though James was quite animated when Alfred first came down and interrupted them. Alfred thinks he hears them whispering to each other. James' words echo in his head. If he found out. If he found out what?

"So what were you guys arguing about?" Alfred calls out. No response. He speaks louder. "What you guys arguing about?"

"We weren't arguing, Alfie," Charlie barks back.

'What were you guys talking about?"

"Nothing important."

Alfred shakes off the last few drops and glances down at his penis. Has it gotten smaller? Do penises shrivel with age? He stuffs it back into his fly and turns and leaves the head. The other two men, sitting at the table, face him. Between them, the liquor bottle is on the table, and so are three shot glasses.

"What's this all about?" Alford asks gruffly as he faces them down.

"You want a drink, Alfie?" James asks. "Sit down and we can do a shot together. Like old times?"

"Stop it, James. Alfie's not allowed," Charlie says.

Alfred recognizes the label, top line Johnny Walker, and he remembers how the three of them used to drink it together with his father, how good it tasted. At the same time, he senses conspiracy in the attitudes of the two men, and the whiskey is simply a ruse to throw him off. "You have something to tell me?"

"Sure, after you have a drink," James replies.

"No," Alfred says reluctantly. "Better not. I promised Kate. What did you guys want to talk about?" He looks from James to Charlie.

"Do we have to sell *Trinity*?" Charlie asks. "She's part of the family by now."

"We've been over this already, Charlie. Dad did not leave enough money. A wooden yacht like this costs a fortune to upkeep, and think of the money we can get for her."

"But if we all pitched in," Charlie says. "James and I were thinking . . ."

"James and you were thinking?" Alfie turns to James. "Was this your idea?"

James shakes his head. "No. Charlie wondered if there was some way to keep the vessel."

"You and Beatrice want to keep her too," Charlie adds.

"But realistically . . ." James shrugs. "I know you're right, Alfie."

"Of course I'm right." Alfred looks back at Charlie. Charlie glares at James. Alfred feels a bit lighter, now the conspiracy is dispelled and James is on his side.

James fills the three shot glasses.

Alfred gets a hint of the whiskey's dark woody aroma, and he steps closer to get a better whiff. "I would do anything to keep the *Trinity*. But it's not feasible. You're smart enough to know that, James."

"Sure you don't want some?" James asks. "A sip won't hurt."

"He can't have one, James," Charlie says.

"Charlie, since when did you poop the party?" James recaps the bottle. "One shot can't hurt. This is a special day."

"I can't believe you already sold the fishing gear," Charlie says.

"Most of it," Affred replies. "Not like we can use it without the *Trinity*, and my buddy Morgan gave the estate a good deal on it."

"I bet he did," Charlie mutters. "A sweet deal for one of your damn Navy friends."

"Jesus, Charlie," Alfred shakes his head. "Why bring this stuff up now? We need to all be here for Dad."

"No arguing." James waves a hand over the three shot glasses. "Let's all drink a toast to Farley."

"I don't know." Alfred looks over at the Johnny Blue longingly. He hasn't touched a drop of booze in seven hundred fifty days; he counts every day since he made that promise to Kate after she walked out on him for a week. On the other hand, they are here to celebrate his father. Johnny Walker Blue is not just top of the line, but the one their dad liked best. "Why the hell not."

I won't even drink the full shot, Alfred thinks to himself, in full control. It's not like either James or Charlie would dare tell Kate or Beatrice. One small sip, no harm in that. It's the noisy bars that make him want more, and this one is for his dad, for this special occasion.

The sip hits his tongue and feels wonderful. He taps the half-full shot glass back on the table and savors the taste, sloshes the liquid in his mouth before he swallows it.

Then he hears feet fall on the steps from the stern. A moment of panic, he thinks it might be Kate or Beatrice. He turns, and relaxes again. It's the other woman, Charlie's girlfriend. Ellie or Evie. Without thinking he grabs the shot glass, finishes the drink. He walks past Evie and up the steps to the main deck where he can hear the gulls squabbling as they dive-bomb the floating debris.

If his father was here, he'd try to pick off a few gulls with his service revolver, a Smith & Wesson Model 10, that Alfred had switched out with his own similar pistol when he woke that morning. Alfred steps to the rail to get a closer look. He did want to shoot off the gun for his father and this is the perfect excuse. He pats at the revolver, beneath his shirt in its holster. Now might be a better time than any.

10: James

"Charlie! You need to look out the window!" Evie points to the round porthole.

"What is it?" Charlie says as he joins her. "That's . . .." His words freeze in his throat.

"Isn't that sick?" she says.

James pours himself another shot of whiskey. Alfred has already started up the steps to the deck. Charlie and Evie have their heads together, looking out the porthole, their arms around each other.

"What is it?" James asks them. They don't answer so he walks over to the other porthole, past the head. He spots the gulls first, swooping and circling, and below, the floating island of trash, about hundred-fifty yards from the boat, and beginning to fall behind, that he has to angle to the side of the porthole to see it. Marine debris, nothing to get excited about. He steps back around to see Charlie and Evie still glued to the porthole.

"It's so sad," Evie says.

James can't hear Charlie's response, which Charlie whispers in Evie's ear.

"Just like some people, Charlie," she says.

"It's nothing," James says to their backs. "Just trash in the ocean."

They don't acknowledge him, as they nuzzle words at each other like he's not there. He shrugs and heads back up to the main deck. Alfie stands at the rail. The gulls and the debris are dropping behind.

"They're making a terrible racket," James says. "Worse than crows."

"I think the animal is still alive," Alfie says.

"Animal?"

"Trapped in the plastic. Maybe a dolphin."

James peers out and can almost make it out, gray and bloody.

James follows Alfie to the rear corner where the main deck thins to a four-foot width next to the bulwark to the helm console. In the side of the bulwark is a door to the storage cabinet where the fishing gear is kept. Or was kept before Alfie sold it, all that is left in the cabinet is one spear gun.

"I can hit it before it gets too far." Alfie pulls back his shirt and pulls the revolver out of the holster.

"You think so?"

"Sure. I might not see as well as I used to, but I can still aim." Alfie points the gun and pulls the trigger twice. Two loud bangs. "See, I hit it. Put that poor creature out of its misery."

"How can you tell?" James asks, still jarred from the noise, a slight ring in his ears. The debris is now two hundred yards behind them, the details blurry.

"What's going on down there?" Kate yells from the helm.

"Nothing. Just shooting at the debris," Alfie yells up.

"Alfie, that gun is not a toy," Beatrice admonishes.

"Maybe you should put the gun away," James says.

"I guess so."Alfie slides the gun back into the holster. "At least it came in handy for something. Don't think we'll need it again, but one never knows. There are pirates, even in these waters. Pirates, smugglers."

"You think so?"

"Bad people everywhere. That's one thing I know from watching the news."

"Maybe it'd be better if you don't shoot anything else," James says.

Alfie looks at him. "It was just for Dad. Remember how he'd take shots at signs and buoys and gulls? At least I know his gun still works."

"Hopefully you won't need it," James says.

"One can never have too many guns in these dangerous times. That's why I decided to hold on to one of the spear guns."

What a stupid thing to say, James thinks. You can only use one or two weapons at a time. Alfie is a full-blown gun nut, owning thirty or more firearms, including a semiautomatic assault rifle. Most of them are locked in a couple steel closets in his basement, which he showed once to James and Charlie, implying they weren't real men because James only owned a couple of handguns and Charlie rejected firearms altogether.

It's an addiction, the need for more and more guns. Not that James would dare bring it up with Alfie.

11: Charlie

In the yacht's cabin, Charlie and Evie stare out the portal. The seagulls dive bomb the animal trapped in the plastic, a seal maybe, Charlie thinks.

"So sad," Evie murmurs.

"The seagulls don't think so. One person's tragedy is another's fortune," Charlie says."Seagulls aren't people, Charlie."

"No. It's sad, what we are doing to our oceans. Just like on land. No escaping the waste. And a poor animal gets trapped in it."

The dead animal and the gulls vanish from view. The sight was disturbing, something you want to turn away from but can't, and now it's behind them. They move away from the window. Her body next to his relaxes, and he hugs her tighter, pulling her around in front of him to give her a kiss.

"We can't let it upset the rest of the trip," he says as he brushes her dark hair back from her face.

"I hope not."

"I'm glad you're here with me," he says, and he kisses her again.

"This really the last time they will have the boat?"

"Yacht," Charlie corrects her. "James agrees with me we shouldn't sell it, but he can't stand up to Alfie."

At the sound of a gun blast from outside the cabin, Evie flinches. Another shot goes off a second later. "What was that?" she asks. "Are they letting off firecrackers?"

"No. Alfie and his damn gun."

"A gun?"

"He carries it everywhere, even on the *Trinity*. He's probably shooting at the gulls. My dad was always shooting off a gun when no other vessels were around." Charlie shakes his head. "Like I said, my family are all a bit off."

"Why does he have a gun?" Evie asks.

"He acts so tough, but he's scared to walk into a grocery store or bar without his concealed carry."

"But he's still your brother, Charlie."

"I never think of him that way. Fifteen years older than me." Charlie points past the berths to the ladder steps at the front end of the cabin. "Have you been to the bow yet?"

"The front? No."

"Let's go." He takes her hand and leads her to the far end of the cabin, past the berth to where a ladder climbs up the wall to a hatch to the bow.

He steps out on the deck and pulls her out as well. The deck is triangular with curved sides where it narrows to a point twelve feet in front of them.

"It's breezier up here than aft," he says. "But it's nice to lounge around. Good place to catch some rays. And we smoke joints, here, where Alfie can't see."

She steps gingerly to the bow, clutching at the rope railing as she looks out at the expanse of sea. She looks so beautiful, he thinks, like the mermaid figurehead on an old sailing ship come to life as she puts a hand over her eyes to scan the horizon ahead. He steps next to her.

"Scary," she says as she grabs his hand, "just that rope for a rail."

"Yeah, we should have life jackets when we're up here. But no one has fallen in whole time my dad owned the *Trinity*."

The yacht holds memories for Charlie. It hints with the creak of the wood beneath them and luff of the sails above their heads. Back when he was young, his mother and his father together, the family out for a sail, the wind blowing in everyone's hair, and him walking around, in the bright orange life jacket that he would pretend was a super hero costume or a jet pack.

"What are you thinking about?" Evie asks, as she pushes past him to get away from the bow, her hand pulling his. She spins again to face him.

"Nothing much. Memories."

"I can't stop thinking about that thing out there."

"That too." The image of the gulls and the dying dolphin intrude on his childhood reverie. "I wouldn't want to fall in. End up like the dolphin," Evie shudders.

"I won't let that happen," Charlie says.

"I don't even know how to . . ."

12: Evie

". . . how to swim," Evie tells him. Charlie'll laugh at her, she thinks. He'll think she doesn't belong on the ship. As they step back from the narrow front edge of the deck, she studies his face for a trace of mockery or derision.

Instead he shrugs and looks at her tenderly. "No one ever showed you how?"

"No. Never learned. I don't even own a swimsuit."

"That's something I can teach you. Before the summer is over."

"Really? I'm not a good student."

"I'm not a good teacher, so it'll work."

She can't help but smile at this remark, and it's enough to push back the edginess that has encroached since getting on the boat. The coldness of Charlie's sister and James. The endless gray-green sea, scary and empty, nothing but sea and sky and them alone, as if the only other thing that exists besides the *Trinity* is the floating island of trash where the gulls slaughter a dolphin.

She pulls him closer. "Do you love me?"

"Of course I love you."

"Tell me again."

"I love you, Evie." He tightens his arms around her and kisses her. "You must know how much I love you." His embrace reassures her, pushes back the shadows of fear and doubt, and when he kisses her again, with even more passion, she can almost forget the world beyond herself and him, as if they could be anywhere and not on the front deck of a large boat, as if nothing else in the world exists at that moment.

"You feel better?" he asks when they end the kiss.

"I think so. You're being nice," Evie says. He probably feels guilty, Evie thinks, for not telling her about his father's ashes until she was already aboard. "I feel like this is a test."

"A test? What do you mean?" Charlie asks.

"One of those tests of a relationship. Will the family approve of me?"

"It's not a test," he says.

"What if they don't, Charlie?"

"They will. Sooner or later. They have to."

"And if they don't?"

"I don't care about them. You are important. Their problem, if they can't accept you, Evie. Not your problem or mine."

"But I want them to like me, Charlie. I want to be a part of this family."

"It might take time. At least there's Kate. You met her in Portland?"

"That's right," she says.

"That's so cool. So what happened?"

"We shared a table at an outdoor cafe. And she started talking to me."

"That's it?" Charlie asks.

"Uh huh." Evie bites her lip to keep from saying more.

"I remember when she went down there. A couple years ago. We thought she'd leave Alfie, find someone new." He looks at her intently. "What is it about Portland and you?"

"What do you mean?"

"You met Kate there. And that other thing you told me about."

She shrugs. "What thing?"

"That time you slept with a woman. The hotel room. That happened in Portland, too."

"What can I say?" Evie pulls away from Charlie and looks towards the rear of the vessel. "We should join the others, don't you think?" She had hoped he'd forgotten that her affair with a woman had happened in Portland.

"Sure. More comfortable on the main deck." He steps past her to the edge of the deck. With one hand by the railing, she follows him along the thin side deck to the rear of the vessel, where Kate and Beatrice sit in folding canvas lounge chairs.

PART II: THE BIKINI

13: Beatrice

On the main deck, the lounge chairs are arranged in a semicircle with Beatrice's chair at the center. "The sea runs in the Mayhew blood," Beatrice says proudly. "Several of our ancestors were whaling captains, and both Alfie and our father were admirals in the Navy."

"Our ancestors ran other cargo too," Charlie says, from a chair near hers.

"Shush, Charlie. We don't talk about that."

"What'd be worse than killing whales?" Evie asks, at the far side of Charlie.

"Charlie, Charlie, always eager to sully the family name," Beatrice chides. "But we have a rule. No talk about politics or religion while we're on the *Trinity*."

"It's not about politics," Charlie replies. "I think it's important to know everything, the good and the bad. No hiding the ancestral skeletons."

"I prefer to be proud of our heritage, Charlie." Beatrice turns to Evie. "How about you, Evie? Do you revel in exposing every bad apple in your family's history?"

Evie shrugs. "I don't know much about my family. Just my mom and me. And an aunt." She glances down at the deck. "We didn't have a father."

"Really?" Beatrice has a pang of pity for Evie. Perhaps that is why Charlie has taken her in, out of pity, his need to fix another life when his own is a frivolous mess.

James steps out of the hatch to the cabin in bathing shorts and flip-flops, with a towel around his shoulders and a bottle of tanning lotion in his hand. "Decided to change," he says. He reaches the empty lounge chair, between Beatrice and Kate and angles it towards Beatrice before he slumps down.

"It is hot," Kate says, standing up. "Think I'll change into my bathing suit too."

"Good idea," Beatrice says. "I'll go down with you." She gets on her feet.

"How about you, Evie?" Kate asks. "Want to come with us? Put on your bathing suit?"

"Bathing suit?" Evie perplexed. "I didn't . . ."

"You didn't bring a suit?" Beatrice asks, incredulously.

Evie shakes her head.

"Give her a break, Beatrice. She's never been on a yacht." Kate turns to Evie. "Charlie should have told you."

"Sure, always my fault," Charlie remarks with a shrug.

"Maybe she can fit in one of my old ones," Kate says.

Who is Kate kidding? Kate is not as slender as she used to be. Beatrice surmises. Evie might be a thin waif now, but give her a few years . . . Down below, Beatrice crosses the cabin to the master berth and shuts the door. She pulls her new swimsuit out of her suitcase and quickly changes into it, a modest one-piece in pink with blue ruffles. She looks at herself in the mirror on the door.

The creaks and groans of the yacht are painful to hear, remembering Alfie voicing concern for the upkeep of the vessel when he assumed his role as the head of the family. Now the repairs are too much, and the *Trinity* strains under the burden of one more passenger than expected.

Beatrice hears the voices of the other two women outside the berth. Curious, she walks to the door and puts her ear to it.

Kate says something and Evie laughs, a trickle of sweet venom from deep in her throat. With her ear to the door, Beatrice can only make out some of the words.

". . . nice of you, Kate."

". . . think about it. Here's one . . . might fit."

". . . ice . . . incident.. sore ear . . ."

". . . fight with a . . . alone . . . underhand . . ." Kate's voice becomes quieter, the words unintelligible.

Evie and Kate continue the conversation in hushed tones, their voices barely discernible through the door. Unable to make out their words, Beatrice opens the door and steps out of the berth.

14: Kate

"Here's one that might fit." Kate hands the bikini to Evie. "Sorry, it's so old. I just found it a couple weeks ago behind the dresser drawers when Alfie and I were cleaning out the *Trinity*."

"Thanks." Evie unravels the two pieces, a look of doubt on her face. The bra section is two purple velvet triangles, each with a bright yellow triangle in the center. The bottom is another pair of fabric triangles attached by a thin band. "You used to wear this?"

"Sure. When I was younger. Twenty years ago."

"There's not much of it."

"You'll look good in it, Evie. You shouldn't be so shy." Kate steps closer and lowers her voice. "Do we have an understanding? About Portland?"

Evie glances at the shut door and lowers her voice too. "I need to tell Charlie sooner or later."

"I wish you wouldn't."

"We don't keep secrets from each other."

"That's best. I wish I could say the same. About secrets. When you get older, there's more to hide."

"I think he'll guess anyway," Evie says. "Put two and two together."

"I wish you hadn't said anything to him." Kate stares at Evie's naked thighs as Evie steps out of her panties. Kate flashes back to Portland, two years earlier, the hotel room, three days and nights. It seemed like a dream afterward on the drive back to Seattle, but now the sight of Evie dredges it up more real than ever.

Evie pulls the bottom part of the bikini up over her thighs. "These are so soft."

"Alfie can't know anything about it." Kate pulls on her own swimsuit, a new one-piece.

"I'll talk to Charlie. Do you think this is too . . .?" Evie blushes slightly as she looks down at herself in the bikini, holding the bra section to her blouse.

"Too what? You look good in it."

"I don't know. I think Charlie will like it, but it's a bit . . ."

"A bit what?" Kate asks.

"Revealing?"

"It did upset the parents when I wore it the first time. They were furious with me, especially Alfie's mother. But they didn't say anything, stiff upper lip conservative rigor, and then Beatrice wore a skimpy one too, and James and his speedo."

"I don't want to cause a scandal."

"You won't. That was over twenty years ago when I first met Alfie. My first few rides on the *Trinity*."

"I guess Charlie will like it." Evie turns her back to pull off her t-shirt and her bra.

Kate steps closer. "Here, let me do that for you." Standing behind Evie, she tightens the strap on the bikini bra. "You and Charlie serious?"

"I love him, Kate. I want to be a part of this family."

Beatrice emerges from the berth in a one-piece swimsuit with frills. "Aren't you two done yet?"

Kate steps back from Evie with a pang of guilt. Quickly recovering, she smiles to Beatrice. "Is that suit new? It's really stylish."

"Thank you," Beatrice beams.

"And I found one for Evie."

Beatrice turns towards Evie. "Where the hell did you dredge that thing up?"

"It fell behind the drawer." Kate points to the dresser along the bulwark. "Otherwise it would've been gone long ago."

"It looks threadbare," Beatrice says.

"Better than nothing." Kate shrugs.

"I suppose it IS better than her wearing nothing," Beatrice chortles. "It'll do for now until Charlie buys her a new one."

15: Charlie

On the main deck, as the three women head down to the cabin, Charlie switches to the lounger next to James. James puts down the bottle of sun lotion he has lathered on his chest, face, arms, and legs. His skin glistens as a coconut sweetness wafts in the breeze. "Something on your mind, Charlie?"

"You and Beatrice need to accept her. Alfie likes her, Kate gets along really well with her."

"Kate gets along with everyone. And Alfie . . ." James chuckles. "He probably wants to jump her pants."

"Shut the fuck up, James. Alfie wouldn't do that. Maybe Dad, but not Alfie."

"Didn't he steal Kate from you?"

"That was long ago." Charlie frowns at his brother-in-law.

"But you're not over it, are you? That's what your sister thinks. You get into these relationships that are doomed to fail."

"Fuck Beatrice and her amateur psychoanalysis." Aware his voice has risen, Charlie glances up at the helm. At the wheel, Alfie stares down with a scowl at him and James. Charlie leans closer to James. "She should examine her own head. Just get her to lighten up when it comes to Evie."

"I'll try, but you know how she is." James points to the flask in Charlie's pocket. "I could use another swig of that."

"Sure," Charlie mutters. He hands the bottle to James, who keeps it under his towel draped over his arm. James steps out of the chair, and in a crouch gets close to the bulwark of the console, out of view of Alfie above, to take a drink from the flask. James returns and hands the flask to Charlie back under the towel, and Charlie pockets it.

"It was crazy for you to bring her on the *Trinity*, Charlie. I wonder if we should let her off at Port Angeles."

"I'm sure Alfie won't mind letting Beatrice off at Port Angeles."

"Stop clowning, Charlie. Not Beatrice. Evie."

"No one's kicking anyone off the *Trinity*."

"For her sake, Charlie," James says. "If she feels uncomfortable, being at this private affair. She might want to get off. You ever consider that?"

Charlie shakes his head. "I want her here. I don't think she wants to get off." Evie so far seemed to be having a good time after a rocky start boarding the vessel, and getting over the fact he hadn't told her about the ashes.

"Charlie!" Alfie's gruff voice cuts through the wind.

Charlie glances up at the steering console. "Alfie?"

"Can you come up here for a moment?"

"Sure." Charlie rises from the chair and James does the same.

"What's up, captain?" James says, following Charlie onto the helm deck. "Need someone to take over the wheel a bit?"

"Listen," Alfie secures the wheel and turns to them. "I saw you down there talking."

"It was nothing," Charlie replies.

16: Alfie

"Nothing?" Alfie snorts derisively as he faces the two men on the helm. More like a mutiny, he thought minutes earlier, as he noticed Charlie and James on the main deck looking up at him surreptitiously, their hushed voices, not laughing loudly about movies and music. And they were more brazen in their drinking, not bothering to go down to the cabin or sitting behind the bulwark on the bow, but instead sneaking sips on the main deck below the helm as if Alfie is a blind fool. "Didn't look like nothing to me. This is our last voyage. So let's enjoy it. And don't forget, I'm Captain."

"We will have a good time," James says. "Unless Charlie freaks out again."

"Stop the bullshit, James. You and Beatrice and your major blow-ups." Charlie retorts back.

"Because you piss off Beatrice."

"Can it, both of you," Alfie silences them. He points to the flask that bulges from an oversized front pocket of Charlie's shorts. "Is that the Walker Blue?"

Charlie nods sheepishly.

"You want another sip?" James asks.

Alfie steps to the edge of the console where he can observe the hatch to the cabin from the corner of his eye. The aftertaste of the Johnny's beckons to him, and once the women return from below, he won't have another chance. A small sip would give him a boost. He knows his limit and he will stop after that. This is a special occasion, the *Trinity*'s final voyage to take his father's ashes to the cove he loved. And the whiskey brings back other memories of his dad.

"Just one sip," Alfie says. "Before the women are back on deck."

"You sure, Aflie?" Charlie asks.

"Come on, Charlie," James says. "Captains orders. Give him another."

"Just one." Alfred reaches towards Charlie. Charlie pulls the flask from his shorts and hands it to him. "This one's the last. And nothing to Kate or my sister from either of you."

"Aye aye, sir," Charlie says.

"Just in time." Alfred hastily hands Charlie the bottle and turns to the movement at the hatch. Is Kate wearing a new bikini? Did she see him hand the flask to Charlie? He squints to get a better look, while he gestures to Charlie to be more discreet, to put the flask away instead of raising it to his lips. They shouldn't have brought the flask to the helm.

The woman in the bikini crosses the main deck towards them. Not Kate at all, Alfred realizes with relief, continuing to stare. The woman's gaze sweeps past the three men, locking eyes briefly on each of them as she steps slowly closer. Alfred remembers how attractive Kate looked in that swimsuit, and how scandalized his mom was.

She climbs up to the console. Alfred turns and sits at the wheel. He pulls off the lines and begins to steer. He relishes the feel of the wheel in his hands, it thrums with subtle power as the yacht harnesses the force of the wind.

"I thought we had some sort of dress code," James remarks.

"Where did you get that?" Charlie asks Evie.

"Kate lent it to me. How does it look?"

"Spin around and let me see."

"Hey, Alfie." James kneels down a few feet away from Alfred.

"What?"

". . . what a thing for her? . . . . .end of us let Charlie stand her . . ."

Alfred barely hears James' whisper. "Huh?" Alfred leans in closer and cups a hand over his ear. "A little louder."

"Praying about their . . ." Eye tat? Lie cat? I can't? James' words lose meaning, erased by the hush of the sea.

"Praying about what? Speak up, James."

"And Charlie sucks at that and singing," James whispers.

"Sucks at what? You make no sense. Speak up!" Alfred twists around to follow James' eyes to Charlie and the girl at the far end of the helm deck.

"Charlie's girl.." James says.

Her name pops into Alfred's head. "Evie."

James moves in closer so that he's less than a foot away, his voice clearer. "The swimsuit, Alfie. What do you think of what she is wearing?"

17: James

James glances to the far side of the console, where Charlie and Evie, their backs to him, look at the vessel's wake and whisper in each other's ears. That bikini, a familiar one . . . where had James seen it before? No one would wear that on the *Trinity*, he thinks. She enjoys standing there, showing almost everything. Maybe James saw it in a porn video?

His anger at Charlie hasn't abated. Ribbing Charlie about Kate jilting Charlie, trying to knock Charlie down a notch, to stop him from acting proud and superior. And he can see his words eat at Charlie. Let him suffer the way he makes James suffer, by bringing that woman aboard.

James slips closer to Alfie at the wheel and leans down to his level, but back three feet where he can view Evie beyond Alfie's shoulder.

"What do you think of her?" James keeps his voice low, so it will not carry to Charlie or Evie at the far end of the deck. "Low class, even by Charlie's standards."

Alfie shakes his head, hand to ear. "Huh? Louder."

"Parading it out there like that."

"Praying about what?" Alfie grunts.

"And Charlie, such a sap he'll say nothing."

"Charlie sucks at what? I can't hear you."

James moves closer, now he sees only her arm and a sliver of her hip past Alfie. "Charlie's girl. Low-class trash."

"Evie. Her name is Evie," Alfie blurts out.

"The swimsuit, Alfie. What do you think of what she is wearing?"

"Yes. Kate's old swimsuit. When Kate could get away with a bikini like that."

James realizes that's why the bikini is familiar. He'd hoped to keep the conversation low, out of earshot of Charlie, but there's no way through Alfie's obtuseness. James is lucky that Evie and Charlie are so locked into canoodling they didn't notice Alfie's outburst. James tries again with Alfie: "It's a bit immodest, don't you think?"

"You think we should keep the *Trinity*?" Alfie asks.

"If we could but . . ." James stammers. "But I know we can't."

"Charlie seemed to think you were with him about keeping her. Second guessing my decision."

"No, Alfie. The woman puts ideas in Charlie's head."

"What ideas?"

"Like he doesn't have to listen to you."

"He never has listened to me. Or anyone else with common sense."

"But . . ." James pauses. Beatrice and Kate step out of the cabin hatch. Might be better if he isn't within eye-shot of Evie dressed like that. As he climbs down to the main deck, he sneaks one last glance at her profile, sweeping from her neck to her toes and back again with a slow nod of his head. He wants to keep that image forever, as he steps on the lower deck and turns to face his wife and Kate.

Beatrice in her new swimsuit settles into a lounge chair. "James, come and join us."

Kate has sat down too. James strolls over with a casual smile.

"Did you see what she's wearing?" Beatrice says. "I hope Alfie gives them a mouthful."

"I didn't notice. Was talking to Alfie." James remains standing.

"It's one of my old suits, Beatrice," Kate cuts in. "Remember when we wore bikinis?"

"But we barely know her." Beatrice reaches into her handbag and plucks out a Kindle.

James considers asking Beatrice again if she wants to take her meds now, and not wait until they reach the cove, but he knows she will get angry if he asks her in front of Kate. He could use another hit of the Johnny Walker and he doesn't want to ask Charlie for it.

"You ladies want anything from below?"

"No, James. We just came from there." Beatrice's tone has a hint of exasperation.

He nods and starts to the hatch. Below, he finds the whiskey in Charlie's duffel and pours himself a double shot and squirrels back the bottle. As the liquid fire goes down, a glow blooms up from his chest to his head, he's had more than he thought. The intoxication is good.

He's still worried about Beatrice not taking her pills. He finds them in the side pocket of her carry-on suitcase and pulls out the blister-pack of tablets, with four pills remaining. She usually took only one unless she started having a hard day. He's not sure if she'll make it before they reach the cove, the signs are already starting to show, her building agitation, the way her eyes begin to dart. Slight variations that he's come to know.

Maybe he can give her a med early without her knowing? Dissolve it in a drink. He breaks a pill out of the plastic blister and walks over to the kitchenette. In the drawer, he finds a fishing knife with a very sharp eight-inch blade. He places the pill on the table and presses the blade on it. The halved pieces fly away. He glances around on the floor but can't find them.

James pulls another out of the blister pack and tucks the pack into the pocket of the suitcase. He'll figure out how break the pill into pieces later. He sticks the pill in his bathing suit pocket. He takes another shot of whiskey straight out of the bottle, and thinks about Evie, on the helm in the bikini, and five nights ago, when she flirted with him across the table, smiling and licking her lips while Charlie sat next to her, unaware. Now, but for three small triangle swaths of fabric, she is naked. Putting it out there to dare him and Alfie and any other red-blooded man who happened to cruise by.

She does it to tease him, knowing he's on a thin leash. Throwing it in his face, making him hate her, and hate Beatrice for keeping him on that leash. Always the tease, see how far it will go. What would have happened that night if those beer glasses hadn't fallen on the floor and woken Charlie? They were all drunk, and Charlie crashed out cold at the table. After all the seduction she threw James, something was bound to happen. Could anyone blame him if he got sucked in? Beatrice could and would, which is why Beatrice could and would never find out.

What could he tell Beatrice? She'd think the worst, though nothing happened, a drunk stupid night, meaningless and not his fault.

Since that night he can't get Evie out of his head. She makes him aware of how trapped he is in his marriage, how the marriage has gone downhill the last several years, and Beatrice's neediness and neuroses has become more pronounced and her looks diminished.

18: Evie

Evie steps out on the main deck in the bikini, feeling more conspicuous in the bright sunlight. As she walks across the deck she is aware of the men's gaze from the helm and she wills herself to look up at them and not at the deck in front of her feet.

Charlie will like it, at least, she thinks. He always tried to get her to wear shorter dresses, more revealing tops, when they went out, always pushing her to be less modest, more daring, to be more comfortable with who she is. She climbs up to the helm and walks over to him, standing alone at the back. "What do you think?"

Charlie looks at the bikini with a slight frown. "That's Kate's old bikini, isn't it?"

"Yes. You like it?"

"I don't know."

"You don't, do you?"

"I didn't say that. It looks sexy on you."

"Kate said it'd be okay, but it is a bit revealing. I thought you'd like it more."

"I do like it. It's nice." He follows this perfunctory statement with a perfunctory kiss on her ear.

The bikini is old, slightly faded, and not the new ones with colors ablaze worn by Kate and Beatrice. Not that Evie minds wearing old clothes. Used clothes are loose and friendly, where as new clothing has a stiffness, and a chemical itch, and when she wears something new, she gets worried about spills or the fabric getting torn on a thorn bush.

"Why don't you like it?" Evie asks.

"It's fine." Charlie attempts a smile. "That was an old me. When Kate wore that bikini."

"What about her?"

"I'll tell you later." He looks past the rail.

"Something happened when she was wearing the bikini. Was it when you went out with her?"

He side-hugs her but keeps looking at the sea with a frown. "No more talk of the bikini. I said later."

"Charlie, are you drunk?"

"Aren't you?"

"I don't know." Evie watches the water turned up to mark the boat's progress before erased by the hungry sea. Words come into her head and she talks more slowly. "The sea catches little bits of sunlight in its constantly changing surface. The rise and fall of the waves, the chaos beneath the ship, the way the sea slaps the ship to remind of its vastness. Holding us above the morass of nightmare creatures from sharks to giant squids to killer whales to Kraken to sinister tentacles and lacy shrouds of poison."

She realizes Charlie is no longer next to her, he didn't stay to listen to her. A dozen feet away, Alfie has the captain's chair swiveled towards her.

He sighs and turns back to the wheel. She sees Charlie on the side deck headed to the front, and she quickly climbs down to the main deck, where Kate and Beatrice sit in lounge chairs. While Evie stands at the bottom of the ladder and considers whether to go with Charlie or join the other women, Kate stands and follows Charlie.

Sucking in her breath Evie slowly walks out onto the main deck. Beatrice looks up at her, a hint of disdain as a wan smile breaks across Beatrice's tight lips.

Evie sits, the lounge chair still warm from Kate's body, and faces Beatrice. Why doesn't she like me? Why is she afraid of me? Evie still smolders from the crack Beatrice made, about Charlie buying her a swimsuit, implying a kept woman, a long-term escort or a greedy tease.

"Hello, Evie," Beatrice says.

"I don't need Charlie to buy me things," Evie blurts.

"I'm sure he buys you lots of things."

"I don't care about that. I love Charlie. He means the world to me."

"Charlie has a history. He's never lasted six months with the same woman."

"I know. I had that problem myself, but we're honest about our checkered pasts."

Beatrice trembles. "Such behavior is far worse in a woman."

"Why should it be?" Evie asks.

Beatrice leans closer, peering at her. "Did he tell you about him and Kate?"

"He said he had a crush on Kate a long time ago. Before she went with Alfie."

"She broke his heart and married his brother. He was eighteen and she was twenty-three. He's never been the same." Beatrice shakes her head.

"That's behind him. He told me about it." Evie picks up a bottle of sun lotion from the deck, squirts some in her hand, and begins to rub it on her legs.

"I wouldn't be too sure," Beatrice says.

"Why are you bringing this up?"

"That bikini reminds him."

"The bikini?" Evie asks.

"The one Kate wore when she broke his heart. It happened on the *Trinity*. Charlie spent the entire trip sobbing below deck."

"Really?" Evie doesn't know if Beatrice is putting her on. "Do you think that's why he's upset?"

"I'm sure of it."

"But Kate must have forgotten. She wouldn't have me wear this if . . ."

"You act like you know Kate when you've barely met," Beatrice says.

"I suppose not," Evie replies, nervous her outburst might give away too much of what Kate wants secret. She lays the sun lotion bottle on the deck.

"The way Kate and you were talking." Beatrice peers more closely at her.

"What of it?"

"It's like you knew each other."

Evie opens her mouth but words don't come. Beatrice eyes her as if to read her face. "You have met Kate before, haven't you?"

"I guess so."

"You either have or you haven't."

Evie nods. "We met once. That's all."

"Is that how you know Charlie?"

"No. Just a coincidence. I met Kate a couple years ago in a cafe." Kate doesn't want anyone else to know. Now she's betrayed Kate, but at the same time she can't lie, Beatrice with her penetrating focus, Evie doesn't dare lie, a lie exposed is worse than the truth.

"A cafe? Really? In Seattle?"

"No. Portland."

"Portland." A frown creeps across Beatrice's face. "When she deserted Alfie in his moment of need? Terrible of her, jumping ship in rough waters. Poor Alfie."

"Maybe she had a reason," Evie says.

"No. There's no good reason when one is married. It's for better or worse. If a wife can't stand by her man when things go bad, she's not a good wife." Beatrice scrutinizes Evie with one arched eyebrow. "If you want to marry Charlie, you better realize the facts."

"I do want to marry him. I love Charlie. And because you're his sister, I want to be your friend, Beatrice."

"Maybe. But you're not part of the family yet. I don't even know why you're here."

"Charlie invited me. But he didn't say anything about your dad. About the ashes."

"That does sound like Charlie."

"I don't even know if I'd be here if he had. I can understand you not wanting me."

"You do understand. That's good." Beatrice's smile seems more genuine. "Charlie's always been a bit messed up. Being so much younger than me and Alfie, it's almost like he's not our brother. Just this little kid that came along after my parents got back together before they split again. I was already twelve when he was born, and Alfie left for the service when Charlie was three."

"At least he has you and Alfie," Evie says. "Sometimes I think I'm missing something, no brothers or sisters, no father. Like I'm not wholly there, and it makes me feel like I don't really understand people. That's why I became a writer. To find that thing I was missing."

They continue to talk. Evie feels like she's broken through to the sister. Beatrice is less uptight as she chats about Charlie and the others in the family.

19: Beatrice

Beatrice feels vindicated. Evie has admitted her mistake of coming aboard. Scattering the ashes was something for the family only. Evie'll be reasonable, and when they dock at Port Angeles, she will probably have no problem getting off. Much relieved, Beatrice chats with the woman, tells her about the family. Evie has very little to say and Beatrice barely comprehends her when she prattles on about a book she read about a missing person. At least now Beatrice can stick with the original plan, no meds until after they scatter the ashes.

"So how long have you known Charlie?" Beatrice asks.

"Since early February," Evie replies.

"Five months? And you live in Seattle?"

"Yes. I moved into his condo a month ago."

"Really?"

"The way rents are in Seattle, and I was over there all the time anyway."

"I can't believe he wouldn't say anything. You two living together. Me and James, we never did that. He didn't move in until we were engaged."

"Oh," Evie's face tightens up, the smile faltering.

"We've been married twenty-two years," Beatrice continues. "People told me I was robbing the cradle, but really he's only seven years younger than me. No one said that to Alfie when he married Kate, and she's younger than James."

Evie turns slightly pale. Beatrice looks up at the sound of footsteps from the bow. Charlie leaps down from the side deck and strides towards them.

"Good to see at least you two are getting along," he says.

"I suppose," Beatrice replies. Evie turns towards Charlie as he moves a lounge chair next to hers and sits down.

Beatrice digests the information in her mind. Living together for a month? And yet James visited Charlie a few days ago and said nothing about Evie living there. Where was Evie that night? Why did Evie flinch when Beatrice mentioned James' name.

Beatrice begins to get that feeling, spiders crawling up and down inside her, that creepy dread that scurries at the corners of her head. She thinks about her medicine, in the cabin below. It's not so bad that she needs a pill, and once Evie is off the *Trinity*, the feeling will most likely subside.

20: Charlie

Charlie steps onto the foredeck and looks out at the empty sea beyond the bow. He wants to be alone for a moment to think. He shouldn't make a big deal of the old bikini but after James joked about what happened twenty-two years ago, that terrible day dredges up from his subconscious as he slumps against the bulwark at the bow.

Twenty-two years ago the *Trinity* sailed from Everett through Possession Sound, the word Possession reverberating in his mind, as he saw Alfie in the captain's seat at the helm and Kate sitting in Alfie's lap, Alfie possessing the girl Charlie loved. Charlie felt like he was falling out of his own
body and off the ship into the ocean, falling deep into its darkness to be crushed by despair at his shattered dreams as he clung to the ladder to the helm.

Then he was in the cabin, curled on his side, vision blurred with tears.

"Charlie, are you okay?" Beatrice asked. Her smug young boyfriend, James, grinned at Charlie, and his father's girlfriend, Tina, didn't bother looking up from her paperback romance.

Farley strode across the deck imperious and proud. "You'll have your turn, Charles. Don't be a crybaby. Want me to give you something real to cry about?" Farley balled his hand in a fist. "We can't have sob babies aboard."

"Maybe we should drop him off at Port Angeles," said one of the women, Tina or Beatrice.

Possession. Possession Sound. The word kept needling him as he lay on the deck in the corner of the cabin, unable to sit up. He hated all of them, their voices barbs that dug into him, taunted him with his loss. Her words worst of all, how could she do this to him, standing over him in that bikini, fake tears in her eyes, I don't want to hurt you, Charlie.

But you are hurting me, just looking at me, your betrayal hurts so deep I don't know if I'll ever recover.

That was long ago. He did recover. He was a different person, he thinks as these memories return. But is he so different? He feels the chasm in his head, threatening to open and pull him in. To see Evie in that same bikini: who will steal his dream this time? Alfie, like before? James? Maybe even Kate, convincing Evie to wear the suit to provoke him and weaken him so that she can take Evie away from him.

It can't happen again. That was twenty-two years ago. He's no longer that scrawny kid, to be taken advantage of. He will fight this time, and not break down, not spend the trip wallowing in grief. He rubs his eyes from the wetness. Maybe a bit of marijuana will help. He pulls out one of the joints as a shadow falls across him.

Kate sits down next to him. "Hi, Charlie."

Charlie lights the joint.

"Something's eating you, Charlie? I see it in your face."

"Is it that obvious?" He hands her the joint. "Why that one, Kate?"

"What one?" She takes a long hit off the joint.

"That bikini?"

"Only one that would fit her. Found it behind the drawer a couple weeks ago. I meant to toss it, but forgot."

"You aren't trying to push me away from her?"

She blows smoke towards his face. "Why would I do that, Charlie?"

"I don't know. I keep thinking about you and her in Portland."

"What about it?"

"The same hotel. The same weekend."

"What are you talking about?"

"Remember? Alfie's spree? I helped you book the hotel."

"So?" Kate asks.

"She said the woman was ten years older than her." He takes a toke off the joint. "Tell me about Portland."

"There's nothing to tell. I was having coffee. She asked to sit down. No free tables. We chatted. We had a lovely conversation, but she walks away and I think I'll never see her again." Kate smiles. "Now, here she is."

"She didn't go up to your room?"

"I don't remember anything like that."

"She didn't spend three days with you?"

Kate shakes her head vehemently. "Listen, Charlie. She's a fiction writer. Her imagination, wild and unhinged. She makes up things, maybe she dreamed it, can't remember what's true or not. It happens."

"Evie doesn't lie to me. I remember when you were in Portland. You didn't call or text for three days."

"I told you, I lost my phone for a day, but I knew it was in the room. I was fine, relaxing, watching movies, and ordering room service. That morning I ventured out for coffee and met Evie. Has Evie said different?"

"I haven't asked her if it was you. But she'll tell me."

Kate takes a hit off the joint and hands it back to him. "You mustn't say anything to Alfie. Any accusations or unfounded insinuations. You know how upset he gets. Are we clear?"

"Sure. As long as you keep nice with Evie. Treat her like family."

"This family treats each other shit." Kate grimaces.

"What do you expect? With my dad?" Charlie rolls his eyes.

"He was a piece of shit, but he knew how to charm."

"If you and Alfie and James treat her well, Beatrice will have to come around. Like with Sally. And Alfie will go along with you."

"You really love her, Charlie?"

"I told you I do."

"I'm happy for both of you. She's a lovely woman."

"I'm glad you like her, Kate."

Kate is about to say something, but she pauses at the sound of the hatch opening. James emerges from the cabin below, steps onto the deck, and shuts the portal.

"I caught that, Charlie," James says while sliding onto the deck between him and Kate. "Setting up a threesome?"

"Not at all," Charlie mutters. Hands shaky, he passes James the joint.

"So, Kate, what do you think of our . . ." A needle of insinuation in James' drawl: " . . .our new guest?"

"Evie? She's okay. And Charlie adores her."

"Not making you jealous?" James asks.

"No, why should it?" She glances over at Charlie with a frown.

"You can tell me," James says. "You know I won't tell Alfie."

"There's nothing to tell," she says. "Why do you think there would?"

"Cut the shit, James," Charlie snaps. "No one wants to hear your innuendos."

"That's why the two of you were up here talking in hushed tones before I showed up?"

"What sort of innuendos?" Kate looks to Charlie.

"Ask James. He likes to make shit up." Charlie pulls himself to his feet. "I'm headed aft."

It isn't the first time James has insinuated Charlie and Kate are having an affair. Two or three times James had brought it up. Charlie is not sure if James is serious or joking. In his current mood, he wants nothing to do with James and his bullshit.

21: Kate

Kate watches Charlie step toward the side deck and head to the rear of the yacht. She thinks about following him, as upset with James as Charlie obviously is, but she wants to find out what James thinks he knows, these innuendos Charlie referred to.

"Well, James? What have you been telling Charlie?"

He shrugs. "Charlie's not good at keeping secrets."

"I have no idea what you are talking about."

"I think you do know what I'm talking about."

She shakes her head. "Spit it out, James."

"What's this about you and Charlie and Evie?"

She shakes her head. "Nothing. Have you had too much to drink, James?"

He takes a long hit off the joint, now just a nub.

"Come on, James," Kate says. "None of that. Are you spreading lies about me?"

"Me?" He takes a few more furious puffs before he flicks the remains near the edge of the deck. "I base evidence on what I see. You are jealous of Evie after your affair with Charlie. Tell me about you and Charlie. I'll keep it from Alfie, from Beatrice. We're not related to this insane clan. Just tell me."

"That was long ago, before I met Alfie. What kind of shit're you percolating?"

"You hid at Charlie's during Alfie's bender two years ago. Everyone knows you did."

Kate shakes her head. "No. I drove to Portland. Stayed in a hotel."

"Come on, Kate. I like you." He puts his hand on her shoulder. "I won't tell Alfie."

Kate pushes the hand away. "You won't because there's nothing to tell." She stands up and heads to the side deck.

He obviously knows nothing of her and Evie, but instead, he invented this other thing of her and Charlie. There was that one night, many years ago, where she and Charlie kissed, a drunken kiss with too much tongue, but that was as far as it went. They pulled away before it went further because Beatrice was banging around in the next room. That and the fling she had with Charlie before she dumped the scrawny high school senior for his brother, a military commander on executive career track twenty-plus years ago. The years have recently not been kind to that choice.

The sexual tension between her and Charlie as he matured never extinguished, a certain muted chemistry acknowledged but never to be acted on. Two years ago, when Alfie was on his bender, she questioned if she married the right brother, with Charlie talking sweetly to her and offering help and a bedroom, and even getting a hotel for her so that Alfie couldn't see it on the jointly-owned credit card statement.

As she reaches the main deck, Kate's thoughts are interrupted by a commotion of raised voices.

"Oh!" Beatrice's voice stabs past the rumble of the sea. "Look at the mess she's made!"

22: Evie

Minutes earlier, Evie is relieved when Charlie comes from the bow and sits on a lounge chair next to hers.

"You okay," Charlie asks.

"I don't know. I felt sick." She points to her bare midriff.

"If you have to, go over the side."

"I think I'm okay." Evie settles in the lounge. "A bit of nausea, now it's gone."

It was when Beatrice mentioned Charlie's condo, and James that it came on, this ill feeling slowly building up inside her. Maybe she's afraid she'll have to lie, the way Charlie told her, that she wasn't there that night five days ago, when she, Charlie, and James went out drinking. She thought she might have to puke, but then it passed.

"There might be some Benadryl in the cabin," Beatrice says. "That sometimes helps with seasickness."

"I was just thinking about that scene in Celine's 'Mort à crédit'" Evie says.

"More Cruddy? I don't know that one." Beatrice replies.

"On a boat going from France to England," Charlie says. "One person gets sick and it makes others sick too until the whole boat is a vomit orgy that goes on for pages."

"Sounds absolutely dreadful," Beatrice sniffs.

"Actually it's darkly funny," Evie replies.

"I hardly think a pop star like Celine Dion would stoop to such degrading depths. You are full of stories, aren't you?"

"Ferdinand . . . Louis Ferdinand," Evie tells Beatrice.

"I don't care what it's for or what's loose," Beatrice replies.

Evie is about to explain when the thing in her stomach comes alive again. She stumbles to her feet but then her stomach overwhelms her and she stumbles as it rises up. The next moment she's on the floor on her hands and knees as the burning vile spews from her mouth and splatters to the deck in front of her.

Evie's head is a roiling sea as on her hands and knees, she stares down at the barf in front of her, a spool of drool leaving a thin line between her lower lip and the puddle.

"Oh!" Beatrice's voice stings past the dizziness. Evie hears Kate's voice too, as she scrambles from the side deck ladder. Her footsteps slow on the deck. No one says anything, but Evie senses their eyes on her as she grovels.

"Is she okay?" The voice far away, de-gendered, Evie's not even sure who speaks it, and aware the question is not spoken to her, but to one of the other observers to her humiliation. She looks up to see Beatrice staring at her in horror. " . . .the mess!"

A hand grabs her shoulder. Charlie pulls her up, and holding her waist, propels her towards the cabin doorway.

"You need rest," he says as he pulls her carefully down the steps.

"I . . . I'm sorry I did that." Evie gasps.

"No. Not your fault," Charlie says. His hand around her shoulder, he half carries her across the cabin floor towards the berth.

"It hit me all at once," she says.

"I got queezy once. Spent half the trip down here. Just try to rest." He lets her slowly down on the bed and sits on the edge, looking down at her.

"Did you puke?" she asks.

"No. That was Beatrice."

"She seemed more upset about the deck than me."

"I think so," Charlie says. "She just didn't know how to handle it." He rummages through his shirt pockets and pulls out a joint. "This might help with the sickness."

She nods.

"Fuck it. We're not supposed to smoke down here, but . . ." He lights the joint and hands it to her. "They all have secrets. James is so full of them, makes him act loony. Beatrice doesn't like people to know about her meds. And Kate. She has secrets too, as you know." He looks at her pointedly.

Evie breathes out smoke and passes back the joint. "I don't want to talk about that, Charlie. I hope you're not upset."

"No. It actually turns me on to think about it. You and her. I hope that doesn't upset you."

"No. We shouldn't think about any of it. For Kate and your brother. For the family."

"The family. You're lucky you don't have that burden. Trying to hold on to a name with history pressing down on it. I think it's what drives them all crazy."

"So you want to escape the family, like Joyce in *Portrait of an Artist*. But you know they will always be there." She waves away the joint. "No more for me." The high potency pot has her beginning to not feel the nausea and embarrassment. Her body begins to melt on the bed. "I need to close my eyes, Charlie."

"Good idea," he says. "I'll take care of the rest of this above," he says, indicating the joint by jiggling it in his fingers. She closes her eyes. His footsteps pad across the floor to the ladder at the front. The ladder creeks as he climbs, followed by the pop of door-mechanism, a slight noise as he steps out, and another pop as the door shuts. As he sits against the outside of the wall, it groans, barely heard over the whines and cries of the insides of the boat, bits of timber from every spot making a creak or dither, and the whir and whispering of the ocean, much closer than the higher decks, the waves with a little more punch so directly beneath her.

She hears the murmur of a far-off voice or two. She doesn't know how long she's laid, a blink of sleep or longer. She feels better. Head clearer, and stomach not racing. She realizes she has to pee. She steps up, and after a moment of dizziness, she walks to the small bathroom cubicle. As she tinkles, she hears footsteps. She left the door an inch ajar.

"Charlie?" she calls out. No, she thinks, the footsteps are from the back, not the front. Kate, perhaps, but the footsteps are determined, loud, the bare feet of a man slapping the floor as he nears. She can hear a duffelbag unzipped and the top of a bottle twisted off. As she reaches for the door James appears outside, looking in at her through the gap.

"Do you mind?" She slams the door on his leer.

James. The last person she wants to see alone. She pulls the bikini bottom back over her crotch and takes a deep breath before stepping out.

"Sorry about that," James says, across the room.

"I don't want trouble, James."

"Me neither. No one wants trouble. We all want to get along."

"Something like that must never happen again, James."

"Hey, we were all drunk. No one to blame."

"You were too drunk. And you are getting drunk now."

He smiles. "I should say the same to you. The way you threw yourself at me in front of Charlie that night."

"I did no such thing," Evie replies.

23: Kate

Kate steps down from the side deck. On the main deck Evie is on her feet, her hands on her stomach, her face pale while Charlie helps her with an arm around her shoulder. A puddle glistens on the deck a couple feet from the railing. Beatrice nearby in a lounge chair has a horrified look on her face.

"Sea sickness, all it is." Charlie leads Evie toward the hatch. "Let me get you into the cabin to rest."

Beatrice glances up at Kate. "Look what she did! All over the deck!"

"I'm sure she didn't mean to," Kate replies.

"The stain it'll leave when we need to sell the *Trinity*"

"It's not so bad, Beatrice." Kate steps closer to the vomit, a slick of yellowish liquid with bits of solid, not quite the size of a seven-inch vinyl single.

"It's making me nauseous. I smell it from here."

"You can't blame her for getting seasick, Beatrice."

"No. I blame Charlie. He should've left her home. I can't relax, with that . . ." Beatrice shudders, and gestures to the puddle.

"I'll get towels from below." Kate walks towards the hatch to the cabins. She reaches it as Charlie emerges from below with a roll of paper towels.

"Is she okay, Charlie?"

"I think so. A touch of sea sickness." He crouches down above the vomit. "She's resting now."

"What's going on?" James calls out as he steps down from the side deck.

"Nothing." Wiping the vomit, Charlie doesn't look up.

"Charlie's girlfriend puked all over the deck," Beatrice says. "Not even the decency to heave h'over the side."

"It's okay, Beatrice," Charlie mutters. "I'm cleaning it."

"A dreadful mess. Some people don't belong on a yacht." Beatrice shakes her head.

"Didn't you get sick first time you sailed?" Kate asks Beatrice.

"I was just a child, not an adult like . . ."

"Give her a break, Beatrice. Evie's never sailed before."

Beatrice narrows her eyes at Kate. "You seem to have taken a gander to her, Kate."

"Not at all." Kate gazes back at Beatrice, trying to stay calm as Beatrice's subtle accusation roils in her head. "I want Charlie to be happy, as I'm sure you do."

"There. No longer exists." Charlie dumps the dirty paper towels over the side.

Kate sits in a lounge chair. James walks over and slumps into a lounge between Kate and Beatrice, while Charlie remains standing, facing them with the rest of the roll of paper towels.

"Are you sure she's right for you, Charlie?" Beatrice asks.

"You ask that, no matter who I'm with."

"Not true. Sally was okay."

"I didn't love Sally. Me and Evie are in love and we're getting married."

"So she said. You really think she belongs in this family?"

"She does if I want her to," Charlie says. "What does it matter to you?"

"Because I'm your sister, Charlie. I want you to make the right decisions."

"You can't tell me what's the right decision."

"The way she flaunts herself in that skimpy bikini," Beatrice says. "James doesn't like it and neither does Alfie. It's upsetting everybody."

"Why do you sabotage any relationship I have?"

"Do you know who she is? How can you trust her?"

"I do trust her. There's no secrets between us."

"How can you be sure? How do you know she's not out to cheat you?"

"I don't have to listen to this bullshit! Me and Evie are honest with each other. Unlike some people." Charlie glares a stink-eye at James, turns, and stomps towards the hatch.

"Charlie? What do you mean by that? Come back here!" Stunned Beatrice watches him skulk away. She shakes her head sadly. "What did he mean? James?"

"He knows he's wrong," James replies."That's why he's so angry."

"But what did he mean by that?" Beatrice turns towards James.

"Mean by what?" The smile slithers off James' face.

"He looked at you when he said it." Beatrice narrows her eyes as she stares at James.

"Said what?" James asks.

"That thing about being honest," Beatrice replies.

"It doesn't mean anything, Beatrice."

"When he said it he looked directly at you, James."

"Me? No." He shakes his head.

"He did too, James. He looked you in the eyes when he said it."

James swallows. "From here it looked more like Kate."

"Leave me out of this," Kate snaps. Watching James sweat bullets to Beatrice's questioning, Kate suppresses a smile.

"Charlie is high, and had too much to drink," James says. "Who knows what he's thinking. And Alfie's calling you."

"Are you hiding something, James?" Beatrice asks.

"No. Damn you, Beatrice! How could you say that?"

"Beatrice!" Alfie's voice hurls from the helm, muffled by wind and age.

"Aflie's probably horrified at her behavior and Charlie's obstinate utterances" Beatrice cones her hands over her mouth and shouts to the helm. "Alfie! I'm coming."

"That's right," James chimes in, wiping the sweat off his face, while Beatrice gazesat the helm. Kate watches them, Beatrice with her suspicions and insecurities, and James, calmer now as Beatrice's attention shifts to her older brother. He risks a look at Kate. "He probably needs another piss break."

"Who? Charlie or Alfie?" Kate asks.

"Charlie's not in his right mind. Alfie needs a man-to-man talk with him." Beatrice, on her feet, heads to the helm deck, her words trailing off. "He's not right. That woman . . ."

"You and me again." Though ashen, James attempts to smile to Kate. "Funny how this happens."

"I think I'll follow her." Kate climbs to her feet. Alfie, lonely at the wheel might be peeved at her for not checking in and now she'll help him get Beatrice out of her lather. Make sure Beatrice takes her medicine. Charlie and James are too drunk and mad at each other.

"What were you all yammering about?" Alfie asks Beatrice as Kate climbs onto the console deck.

"It's nothing, Alfie," Kate steps up beside Beatrice at the edge of the console where Alfie in in profile in the captain's chair.

Alfie glances over as he steers. "Not nothing. I want to know."

"Just Charlie, getting angry at everyone," Beatrice says. "You need to talk to him Alfie, the way Dad would. A man-to-man talk. Tell him this girl is not right."

"Just because she got seasick?"

"No. She's not . . . she doesn't fit in with the family."

"Watching her puke her guts was pathetic," Alfie chuckles. "A sailing disgrace."

"That's what I mean." Beatrice lights up. "She's not a yacht person."

"Neither are we after we sell the *Trinity*."

"That's not the point, Alfie. Charlie is out of his mind as if we're to blame for that girl getting grossly sick all over the deck."

"I remember, first time the *Trinity* sailed, you threw up, Beatrice."

"But I did it off the side. Not all over the deck."

"No. Same place as her. Didn't make it to the rail either."

Beatrice sniffs loudly. "That's not how I remember it."

24: James

"Me and Evie are honest. Unlike someone!" Charlie's anger, his hateful gaze, directed squarely at James. Charlie stomps away, leaving James to deflect a grilling from Beatrice. Why the hell did Charlie do that? And Beatrice, without her meds. She has to stir up trouble, pushing and pushing until Charlie loses his shit.

The panic rises as James faces his wife and tries to push the curse on someone else, Kate, back to Charlie. That's what Charlie put on him, a curse. Beatrice is ready to give James a Spanish Inquisition-styled third degree, her face contorted with suspicion, eyes unblinking as she stares at James. She doesn't even hear Alfie yell her name until James mentions it, and Alfie calls it out again.

It breaks the spell. She turns to go up to the helm. Feeling weak, relieved that Beatrice is out of his face, but more furious than ever at Charlie, James gasps a deep breath. He needs to figure out a way to get Beatrice to take the meds. No way will she last until the cove. He still has a pill in his pocket. He turns to Kate, thinking she can help him, but she follows Beatrice to the helm.

Maybe James can dissolve it in one of her diet sodas. Uncap the bottle and . . . He heads down the steps to the cabin and helps himself to some of Charlie's whiskey, taking a big swallow out of the bottle. That's when he hears Evie's voice. She left the door to the head ajar. He walks over to look in on her before she shuts it. He waits nervously, feeling like a teenager with their first crush. She soon emerges, standing in front of him. Alone with her, a rush of feelings fills his head, the desire he has for her, and the terror if Beatrice finds out.

That night at Charlie's, he can't forget about it. Even though nothing happened. As much as she and he wanted it. He had her pinned to the kitchen counter.

She didn't scream. She wanted some. Her guy face down on the table fast asleep in the next room, but that didn't stop her. Find it somewhere else, gaze aimed at James while James valiantly held off her entreaties until his manhood could take it no more. It was too late, she pulled him to the point of no return as she leaned against the counter. She feigned confusion, didn't resist when he came in closer and closer. She wriggled seductively when he pressed himself against her, her arms to the side, and his around her, and she was making little noises like she wanted it, and his arm must have bumped into the trio of beer glasses. An asinine move, the abrupt shatter of glass unfortunately woke Charlie.

"What was that?" Charlie asked, groggy but awake.

"James knocked over those glasses on his way out the door," she lied.

"Don't worry about it, James. I'll have Evie clean it in the morning."

"Both a maid and a whore," James chortles under his breath.

"What's that?" Charlie asked.

"On my way to the door. See you, Charlie." James stumbled down the steps of the condo, and up the street to his car. That was close. Charlie was lucky those beer tumblers broke in pieces and not his heart. Maybe James and Evie are lucky too. James knows it and she knows it. They have that thing between them, this secret from Charlie, when she and Charlie rave about being so honest as if the rest of the family are contemptible liars.

Maybe Evie's a risk-taker, only wants to fuck when the stakes are high. She probably hoped for a fight between him and Charlie that night. Or maybe Charlie had her lure him on to get him into a three-way with her and Charlie. Charlie would put up with that shit, make a cuck of himself, virtual signaling the way liberal media has brainwashed him. Doesn't care if she sleeps around so he can keep porking Kate on the side because the Captain is not so limber in the timber, and a bit blind. As if Beatrice is the only one in the family who is fucked up.

This time James will be strong. He doesn't know if he should kiss her or slap her, give her a hug, or shake her and tell her to stop playing games with him. But she would only lie and deny she's playing them.

"Don't lie. I know we both want this, Evie. Maybe later?"

She splays her arms at her sides which makes her breasts swell as she looks directly at him with her fuck-me-don't-fuck-with-me eyes. She flaunts her near-nudity at him, trying to make him as naughty as her. "What are you talking about?"

"Charlie not enough for you?"

"Shut up!" she hisses. Her face twists in emotion. Her eyes dart around to make sure they are alone. She doesn't slap him or run away. She's daring him because she likes risk. Dangerous, rough, one of those girls. Let you do things to them. The sex, he imagines, far better than what he gets from Beatrice. The hushed sweetness of her voice, compared to his wife's nag tones.

The thought of Beatrice is absolutely revolting as he stands so close to Evie.

He can barely hear her voice. "I want to put a fence between you and Beatrice," she whispers. "Go try anything!" Her fingers at her side move in and out in a fist as if giving a hand-job.

"You want me in trouble, don't you?" James says.

25: Evie

"I want to be friends with you and Beatrice," Evie says, terrified. "Don't try anything!"

"You want me in trouble, don't you?" Standing over her, James leers at her, mouth drooling.

"No! You're doing it yourself." Evie says.

"I won't fall for it. Not now. Too risky,"

"Someone's coming." Evie hears a door creak. Reason and fear return to James as he hears it too.

"Listen." James leans forward to whisper wetly in her ear. "Not a word of this. Our little secret. Just having fun. Right?" He steps away and she lets out a breath.

She glares at him. She wants to hit him, but her hands continue to tremble at her side as if paralyzed, fingers flailing back and forth. The arms are numb and the hands don't belong to her. James steps away. She turns towards the footsteps.

"Alfie!" James calls out.

Alfie's flip-flops double slap across the floor. He looks at her and back to James. "I don't want to know," he mutters gruffly. He vanishes into the bathroom and slams the door.

Evie takes several deep breaths. James is a dozen steps away, at the far side of the room.

"Nothing going on here. Right, Evie?" A wan smile pulls at his lips.

"Don't ever do that again."

"We can continue another time."

"Never. Or I tell Beatrice."

He smirks. "Beatrice won't believe you."

"Are you so sure?" she asks.

He narrows his eyes and squeezes his lips, unable to reply. She grimaces and heads up the ladder to the front deck, where Charlie last went. She needs to tell Charlie. But then she will have to tell him the last time, and maybe he'll wonder why she didn't tell him earlier as if she held back on the story, keeping it from him for an ulterior motive.

She climbs quickly up the ladder to the bow, at any moment expecting James to grab her ankle and pull her back down. She imagines his creeping eyes staring at her. She steps onto the deck and blinks in the bright sun. Charlie is no longer on the front deck. By herself, the deck feels perilous, the tapering sides and the thin rope rails. She falls against the side of the cabin and takes a deep breath.

The memory of the first time, five days ago, floods into Evie's mind, sharp and clear and suddenly, as if it had built up strength with all her effort to suppress it. The three of them had returned to Charlie's after hitting two bars. They were having fun. She returned from the bathroom, and Charlie was passed out on the table in the next room. James pushed back his chair and stood.

"Guess the party is over," she said to James as she grabbed the three empty beer glasses and brought them to the sink.

"It doesn't have to be."

"What is that supposed to mean?" She placed the glasses on the counter near the sink.

"It can mean what you want it to," James said.

She turned. He stood a few feet away from her.

"I'm tired, James. It's late."

"We've been having such a good time, Evie. Maybe a kiss good night?"

"What?" she asked confused.

"I know you want to."

James, you're drunk," she protested.

He stepped close in front of her. She backed into the counter. He pinned her to the counter with his body. Over his shoulder, Charlie dozed.

James told her not to make noise, it would be their secret. Appalled, she froze. He pushed himself into her against the counter. She wanted to strike back but her hands were helpless at her side.

"Isn't it time you leave, James," she choked from her half-paralyzed lips.

"You don't want me to leave, do you?" he said.

"Yes. I do."

"That's not what your eyes are saying. Inside you want it, but you're afraid to ask for it. So you tease and tease."

"You're crazy, James."

"Me? You should talk. You lured me into this."

"You're delusional, James."

"You act so innocent. But you want it."

Panic rose up inside and gripped her. He put a hand over her mouth and held her shoulders and pressed himself into her. Charlie snored, head on the table. The three beer glasses, set in a triangle on the counter next to her. She elbowed the glasses off the counter. Glass shattered loudly to pieces.

The abrupt noise awakened Charlie. James jolted away from her. She stepped away from the broken glass. Charlie, muddled with sleep, pushed off the table. She told Charlie that James knocked the glasses off the counter while heading to the door. She didn't know how to tell Charlie what really happened. It was something out of control, and maybe James didn't meant it, he was too drunk. A bad mistake after what had been a fun night.

But the beer glasses were in pieces on the floor and James was gone. It was a weird moment, and she didn't want to think about it as Charlie and she went to bed after Charlie slammed the door on James. Forget and pretend it's a bad dream, a mistake, a fucked up move that will not happen again.

Now James strikes again. She can't shrug it off as an anomaly. She is stuck on the boat with a man who wants to harass her, maybe even rape her. Was it all just a joke, as he claimed? What would he have done if she hadn't woken Charlie knocking the glasses to the floor? How far would he take this "game" as he called it.

She stands up and looks across the top of the cabin to the rear of the vessel. Charlie is at the steering wheel; he waves when he sees her.

Evie takes a deep breath and takes several steps towards the bow. The ocean is more raw and feral, overwhelming in its vastness. She looks back at Charlie. Charlie beckons her with his hand. She nods and starts down the side deck.

26: Alfie

Alfred at the helm feels that niggle at his bladder again, so soon after the last piss. He battens the wheel with lines. He climbs down to the main deck. Beatrice and Kate are in the lounge chairs when he could've sworn it'd be James and Charlie. Beatrice speaks quietly and quickly in Kate's ear, and the only words Alfie can make out are "Charlie's girl."

"Alfie?" Kate asks, getting on her feet. "What's going on?"

"Nothing. Just need a bite to eat. Want anything?"

She shakes her head.

"Alfie?" Beatrice stands as well, and steps in front of Kate. "We're nearing Port Angeles."

"What of it?" He puzzles for a moment. As if he doesn't already have too much on his mind. "You want me to let you off before we do the ashes?"

"Not me."

"James? Fine with me."

"Not James, Alfie! Charlie's girl."

"She getting sicker?"

"You don't know how sick." Beatrice's lips quiver speckled and splattered with spittle. "We can drop her off at Port Angeles."

"If that's what she wants." Shit, he thinks, we'll have to change course.

"She has said no such thing," Kate says.

"She did to me, Kate," Beatrice replies.

"Really? We should ask her again to make sure," Kate snaps back.

"Your high-pitched yammering is like magpies." Alfie takes another two steps to the cabin. "Are we veering off to Port Angeles?"

Kate and Beatrice speak up at once. "Yes." "No."

"No one wants to get off," Kate says.

"But if the rest of us decide," Beatrice says.

"No one gets off unless they want to. You two need to man the helm." Alfie points up behind him. "Decide among yourselves whether we stop at Port Angeles."

They give him those queer looks, both his wife and his sister. He realizes he's too shit-faced to answer them, he really has to piss bad, the whole lower guts screaming for bladder release. He turns his back on them and heads to the hatch.

As he steps into the cabin he hears noises. The blurred images in front of him separate as he nears and focuses. James in his bathing trunks looks at Alfred sheepishly, hiding his fear, and Charlie's woman, in that skimpy suit, her face pale and guilty. James prattles off a blandishment.

She says nothing.

Wasn't James saying things about her earlier, trying to provoke a reaction from Alfie as he talked about her? And now here is James, all prepared to cheat on Beatrice with her. That's what it looks like, but Alfred is not sure, and as Captain he can only base decisions on facts.

Besides his bladder is killing him. He rushes into the head. How good it feels to let the urine pour out. The trickle is thinner than normal. Always a little thinner, sneaking up on you like everything else with old age. His father warned him of this. As the urine pitters on the metal, he thinks of what he will say to James or the woman. He should give them both a scolding. What is James thinking, cheating on his wife with his wife's brother's girlfriend? Alfred could fucking ring James' neck for that.

But worse if Beatrice finds out. What has happened can not be undone. Better for Beatrice not to know. They can at least wait until they are on shore, and James and Beatrice can sort the shit out between them. Not in the confines of the *Trinity*. But really, Charlie is at fault too, and the loose woman he brought. If not for her, would any of this have happened?

The urine pitters slowly on the metal, each plink a note on an atonal dirge. He prepares himself to step out of the head. Will James or the girl be in the cabin? Most likely they'll both be gone. That would confirm their guilt. Run away instead of facing up to him.

And if they were both still there? That might mean they are innocent, not afraid of questions, or it might further incriminate their guilt, show their complicity.

What if Charlie's woman is in the cabin alone? Evie is her name? Alfie would have to give her a strong warning. Be polite at first, but let she know her behavior with James is unacceptable. Hopefully Beatrice is right that the woman wants to get off at Port Angeles before they scatter the ashes.

Alfie imagines stepping out into the cabin and finding her by herself in her skimpy bikini. Will she try to make excuses when he confronts her? Or maybe try to seduce him, to get him to say nothing happened? He's not even sure what he'd do in that case. Or will she break down and cry, realizing her terrible mistake? And if she should need a shoulder to cry on. Alfred would be there.

He'd make her tell him what she and James were up to. He would use force if he had to. Hold her to the bulkhead. Make her promise to never do anything like that again. But what if she . . . what if she . . . He stares at himself in the mirror. He's not sure what will happen if he's alone with her. The alcohol puts crazy ideas in his head.

Alfred emerges from the head. The cabin is empty. He saunters to Charlie's duffelbag near the dinette table, where the neck of the Johnny Walker pokes out. He pulls loose the bottle and shakes it back and forth. Almost empty, just a shots-worth at the bottom. He uncaps the bottle.

"Alfie!" James' voice startles him. James steps out of the berth.

"There you are," Alfred says. "What's going on?" He peers into the berth but doesn't see Evie.

"Nothing. Looks like you've almost finished that." James points at the bottle.

"No. Barely had a drop." He takes a couple steps towards James. "Didn't look like nothing going on."

"Not much left." James holds out a hand. "I might as well polish that off."

"Don't change the subject. What were you and she doing down there?"

"Let me have that and I'll tell you." James reaches for the bottle.

"Haven't you had enough?" Alfred pulls the bottle away.

"You're drunk, Alfie."

"You've had more than enough." Alfred raises the mouth of the bottle to his lips. The whiskey splashes into his mouth, a fair bit more than a shot, filling his mouth with heat and volatility, oozing warmth down his throat as he swallows. The whiskey is delightful, but he relishes more James' anguish not getting the last drink.

James stares at him, mouth agape. Swinging his arm to the side, Alfred tosses the empty behind him and hears it clatter unbroken against the deck.

"You something to tell me?" He steps within arm-reach of James, his hands at his sides, ready to go.

James clenches his fists and shakes his head.

"You and that girl?" Alfie says.

"No. I'd never cheat on your sister." James twists up his face. "That girl . . . she tried to . . . You see the way she is, Alfie."

"You do anything to hurt Beatrice . . ."

"I never would. Talk to Charlie." James looks like he's ready to cry. "We need to let her off at Port Angeles."

"What if she doesn't want to get off?" Alfred asks.

"We'll take a vote. Her loose behavior, maybe even Charlie will agree. And you as captain wouldn't be blamed."

"We're not voting anyone off the *Trinity*," Alfred says. "This isn't a reality show. Or a democracy. I'm captain."

"I know, Alfie, but for the good of the journey . . ." James pleads.

"Are you telling me what to do?"

"No, no, of course not, Alfie. You're the captain."

"Don't forget it. And stay away from that girl." Alfred heads to the helm.

"Get her off the *Trinity* and I will," James mutters under his breath.

Alfie spins back. "What's that?"

"Nothing."

"Nothing?"

"Nothing, Captain, sir!"

Alfred glares at him. "Don't think I like the cut of your jib, James."

As Alfred heads aft, he wonders if James mocked him with that "Captain, Sir." What was James doing down here with the woman? It seemed wrong when Alfred first entered the cabin, them moving away from each other caught in the act. At one time he trusted James but recently he'd begun to worry, when James asking him what he thought of the girl earlier, and now this.

At the same time, she's also to blame. No doubt she'd lure a weak-willed man like James. Maybe Alfred will tell Charlie to reign her in. Warn Charlie about her. What a damn mess. Alfred sighs as he emerges into the sunlight on the main deck.

He'll feel better once he's behind the wheel. And what was that second bottle in Charlie's bag, which James pulled out and opened? A brown fluid in a clear roundish bottle. Not that Alfred wants any. Nothing is as good as Walker Blue. But the label of that second bottle is still in his head. Balvenie triple cask 16-year single malt. A scotch Alfred's never tasted, a scotch too expensive even for his father. One of those single malts spoken of in hushed voices in wood-paneled cigar rooms. Where the fuck did Charlie steal that stuff?

Alfred stumbles on a step to the helm, but fortunately no one notices. As he climbs to the deck, he sees Charlie and Evie at the wheel, her sitting on his lap while both have hands on the wheel.

"Fuck, Charlie! You need to be alert! This isn't a hotel room."

Evie startled, squirms off of Charlie and the seat.

"Two sets of eyes, better than one." Charlie shrugs and stands slowly to face Alfred. "You okay, Alfie?"

"Why wouldn't I be? You sure you're okay?" Alfred sits down in the captain's chair. "Charlie, I need to talk to you."

"Go ahead, Alfie. That's what we're doing."

Alfie secures the wheel and half-swivels to Charlie and the woman, six feet away.

She tugs on Charlie's arm. "Charlie, should I go down?"

"Yes, go down." Alfie pauses and clarifies. "Down to the other deck."

"Alfred, you can't share with Evie too?"

"Me and you alone." Alfred's jaw hardens as he glares them. Their innuendos, going down on someone and partner sharing. Charlie always the joker. When will Charlie grow up? And Evie joining in, provoking Charlie.

Alfred coaxes Charlie closer with his finger. Charlie steps to the edge of the steering wheel housing. When Charlie was younger, he'd kneel to Alfie's level when the two of them had talks up here. The same way they both knelt to their father when he was at the wheel. But this time Charlie remains standing, his hands folded over his chest, his skin glistening with oil in the bright sun.

"What's up, Alfie?"

Alfie gets to his feet to face Charlie. Alfred realizes his brother is the same height as him. Alfred keeps his voice low. "You need to watch your woman."

"What are you talking about, Alfie?"

Alfred clears his throat. "I think she's hankering for your brother-in-law."

"James?" Charlie grins and shrugs. "No way! Who the hell is telling you this shit?"

"Don't be so smug, Charlie."

"We love each other, Alfie. I trust her."

"That's what you said before. Those other women."

"Never said that before. None of those girls . . ."

"You dump them before they dump you. But I know how you get when they dump you. I've seen it."

Charlie scowls. "You're bringing that up?"

It's mean of Alfred, but he does it to throw Charlie off. Make sure Charlie knows who's in charge.

"Charlie? I don't want trouble with Beatrice. You talk to her. Talk to James."

"You talk to them," Charlie counters. "Tell them to stop meddling. And you? Take me seriously for a change."

"How can I, the way you act?"

"Stop listening to Beatrice. Is she telling you lies?"

"It's nothing Beatrice said. It's what I saw."

"What did you see?"

"That woman and James. Down in the cabin."

"I don't believe you, old man."

"I know what I saw."

"You're drunk, old man." Charlie clenches a fist.

Again with the old man. Alfred flinches at the sting of his brother's words. "Don't talk to me that way! Do I need to slap some sense into you!"

"You can fucking try!" Charlie trembles as he says this.

"I'll fucking deck you, Charlie. Don't make me do it."

"Go ahead."

Alfred takes a deep breath and lowers his voice. "Listen, Charlie. I don't want any problems. I'm just telling you what I saw."

"I don't need your bullshit," Charlie says loudly and storms to the ladder. Alfred shakes his head, upset with Charlie's insubordination, worse than James. If it gets any worse . . . Alfred gazes down at his clenched fist. He should have decked Charlie then and there with that "old man" crack. The nerve!

Alfred almost stumbles as waves jostle the *Trinity*. The helm deck under his feet undulates with the sea, the sails massive walls of a white wave that never seems to fall. He falls into the captain's chair and grabs the dashboard to steady himself. He slumps against the wheel with his eyes closed. It's nothing, just the booze. Take some deep breaths. He tightens his body and opens his eyes.

Strength trickles into him as he pulls off the lines and takes the wheel. No more alcohol for him. The bottle of Johnny Walker is empty. No more whiskey. He imagines a bottle afloat on the sea. But he remembers the other bottle. He pulled it out of Charlie's duffel bag earlier out of curiosity. A squat bottle with a roundness on the neck, a bottle full of yellowish-brown liquid, an ocean of it in the bottle. He's never tried a sixteen-year single malt. It might be the thing to jolt his head into focus, the bracing simplicity of a single malt.

27: Charlie

Charlie faces off with his older brother on the helm. "I don't need your bullshit!" Hands clenched, Charlie suppresses the urge to swing at Alfie, an act he'd never dare a few years ago. He even thinks he can best Alfie in a fight. You won't call me wuss again.

This revelation stuns Charlie. His older brother in front of him, a weak old man. A drunk old fool. How did this happen? Unnerved, Charlie turns and walks to the ladder down to the main deck. Alfie calls after him.

Charlie needs time to think. As he steps on the main deck Kate rushes past him to climb the ladder to the helm. They exchange angry words. He tells her Alfie is drunk and she looks mortified as she clambers up the ladder to her husband.

Charlie looks out at the gray emptiness of the Salish Sea. What kind of bullshit was Alfie feeding him, about seeing James and Evie in the cabin? Did Beatrice twist Alfie against Evie with her lies? Or maybe Kate's the culprit, tricking Evie into wearing that bikini.

Alfie isn't one to make up gossip or tell lies, though he will believe the lies of others. He said he himself saw something. James and Evie together? Probably nothing, Charlie thinks, and yet it niggles at him. Evie said nothing about it. Maybe she hadn't had a chance.

But Evie would have said something. Twenty minutes earlier she seemed distraught when she walked over from the bow, and Charlie wanted to comfort her. She reluctantly agreed to sit in his lap. He apologized for his family's behavior, and she brushed it off, saying it was okay. He could tell she was nervous at his public display of affection, pulling her in for a kiss, and he realized he was only doing it for himself, to change an old story.

"Should I wear something else?" she asked.

"No. You look good in that bikini. Silly of me to be upset."

"But if it reminds you of . . ."

"No." Over her shoulder Charlie saw Alfie below emerge from the cabin, approaching across the main deck. Alfie would be pissed, returning to the helm, to see them making out in the captain's chair. Alfie considered the helm his domain when their dad became too sick. He, Charlie, in the captain's chair with Evie in his lap, to wash away the memory of seeing Alfie in the chair with Kate in his lap twenty-two years earlier. Between that and standing up to his brother . . . but Alfie's words pull him down. What did Alfie say about Evie and James? And why hadn't Evie said anything about it when she was with Charlie several minutes earlier?

As Charlie looks out at the sea, he thinks how he brought Evie to make the trip easier to deal with. Someone to share it with, someone not in awe of Farley like everyone else, someone on his side. Instead Evie's presence has turned the trip into a shit show. James turning against her when the three of them had a good time days earlier. Kate tricking her into wearing the swimsuit. And now Alfie . . .

But James, it all started with James. Charlie takes a deep breath of the salty air, and turns from the rail. Across the deck, Evie sits up in a lounge chair, staring at him questioningly and beyond James and Beatrice, at the far rail, look out over the water.

"Charlie?" Evie calls out.

Charlie ignores her as he strides past her to the others at the rail.

28: Kate

On the main deck Kate and Beatrice are in the lounge chairs. Kate has in her lap a seven-hundred-page historical novel set in England in 1500, and she's still on the first page where a man lies beaten up on the cobbles. She looks up to see Evie emerge from the side deck.

"How are you feeling?" Kate calls out.

Evie nods "Better, thanks."

Beatrice glances up from her Kindle. "Sure you don't want to get off? We can stop in Port Angeles. There's a bus back to Seattle from there."

"No. I think I'm good." Evie pads past them towards the helm where Charlie steers the ship.

"That's settled," Kate says to Beatrice.

Beatrice sighs. "I guess so. I suppose it's not her fault."

"You should get to know her, Beatrice."

"I know. I wish circumstances were different. Charlie springing her on us like this. Confined to the *Trinity*." Beatrice lays her Kindle on the deck beside her lounge chair. "I just don't know about her."

"What don't you know?" Kate asks.

"If she's right for this family. Is she right for Charlie."

"That's Charlie's choice." Kate glances up, to see James come out of the cabin and walk to the rail. His back to them, he looks out at the water. Kate's anger at him flares up, but she says nothing to Beatrice. Beatrice glances up to see James.

"Why did Charlie say that?" Beatrice asks.

"Huh?" Kate shakes her head, confused.

"He said he wasn't a liar, like some people. And he looked right at you and James."

"He wasn't looking at me," Kate replies. "Sometimes James is a little loose with the truth."

"James?" Beatrice looks confused. "Why would you say that? Surely you mean Charlie."

"Charlie? No."

"Charlie's not rational," Beatrice says. "You always defend his stupidity, Kate. You want to make up for your own guilt."

"Guilt?"

"At what you did to him."

"That was long ago. Why bring that up?" Kate asks.

"That why you're so nice to her?"

"What are you talking about?"

"Nothing is right," Beatrice says. "Even Alfie's acting strange."

"Alfie?" Beyond Beatrice's shoulder, Kate notices Evie at the bottom of the ladder to the helm, standing and staring at her and Beatrice.

"You didn't notice?" Beatrice asks.

"No. What do you mean?" Kate realizes she hasn't paid much attention to Alfie, with everything else that has happened. Evie looks at them nervously, still by the ladder to the helm.

"I don't know," Beatrice mulls. "He's acting . . . Not serious enough, considering we're scattering Dad. He hasn't started drinking again?"

"Alfie? No!" Kate shakes her head. "Of course not."

"Kate, Kate," Beatrice tsk-tsks. She sits upright, glances behind her to see where Kate is looking, and then turns back to Kate. "She's spying on us," Beatrice whispers to Kate.

Evie walks hesitantly towards them, pulls a lounge chair close to Kate's, and sits down."Kate?"

"What is it, Evie?"

Evie lowers her voice. "Why did you have me wear this bikini?"

"Only one that would fit you," Kate replies.

"But Charlie. It's upset him."

"I don't know why it should. Too revealing?"

"No. Beatrice says it reminds him of you."

Kate shrugs. "It was my bikini, so . . ."

"When you broke up with Charlie," Evie says.

Kate sighs "I thought Charlie was over that years ago. It wasn't much to begin with to get over. He didn't take a hint. He was upset that one trip. Spent most of it curled up down below."

"Down below?" Evie asks.

"Yes. In the cabin. The time I wore that bikini. I was worried about him, but to be honest, I was in love and oblivious. But that is the past. He's grown up and left that far behind."

"Are you trying to drive Charlie away from me?"

"No. Of course not, Evie." Kate pats her hand on Evie's arm. "Why would I do that? I want you and Charlie to be happy. I care about you both."

"Do you still have a thing for him like James says?"

"A thing for who? Charlie?"

"Yes. Charlie."

Kate is mortified. "Me and Charlie? What're you talking about?"

"James said something about it."

"James is full of shit," Kate remarks. "His lies can't get back to Alfie." Her hand squeezes Evie's. "I can trust you, can't I?"

Evie nods. "You might be my only friend here. Besides Charlie."

"Shh!" Kate puts her finger to her lips. Beatrice has joined James at the rail. Their voices are loud enough for Evie and Kate to hear, the way the wind carries the words to them.

"What are you keeping from me, James?" Beatrice asks.

"Nothing. Nothing at all." James stammers.

"Charlie pointed at you when he said it. Tell me the truth."

"Why don't you ask him? He's been making shit up ever since . . ." James turns and glances across the deck at Evie and Kate.

"Are you telling the truth, James?" Beatrice peers closely at him while he stares helplessly back.

He closes his eyes and opens them again. "Why don't you trust me, Beatrice? I would never lie to you."

For a moment Beatrice and James are quiet, as they look out at the ocean. Up on the helm, Charlie's angry voice bursts, loud enough to be heard on the main deck. "I don't need your bullshit!"

"Charlie!" Alfie shouts back.

"What's going on up there?" Evie asks Kate.

Kate drops her book on the deck and gets to her feet. "I don't know. I need to check on them. They shouldn't get so heated up there."

Kate hurries towards the helm. Charlie climbs down as she reaches the ladder.. "What's going on?" she asks.

"Your damn husband is making shit up," Charlie mutters.

"Alfie? Why would he do that?"

"Because he's . . . glug glug?" Hand to mouth a drinky motion.

"Drunk?" Kate stares at Charlie. Is he saying that because he's angry? "Alfie can't be drunk," she says. Yet both Beatrice and Charlie have now accused Alfie of drinking.

"He is." Charlie turns from her to look out at the ocean.

Alarmed, Kate clambers to the helm. Alfie seated at the wheel doesn't look up when she calls out his name, approaching him. He looks straight ahead, over the wheel towards the bow. "Alfie?"

"What is it, Kate?" he grumbles, still not looking at her.

"Have you been drinking?" she asks.

"Of course not."

"You have, haven't you?" Kate steps closer. "Don't lie to me, Alfie." She can now smell it on him.

"Just a tiny bit. I'm not drunk."

"You shouldn't have any. Why were you and Charlie fighting?"

"Because he's an idiot," Alfie snorts.

"How much did you have?" Kate asks.

"Huh?" he asks.

"How much did you drink?"

"Not much. You should be asking Charlie. And James." He continues to stare ahead.

"Alfie, look at me!"

"I'm steering the yacht. Stop bothering me."

"You're drunk!"

"You're drunk and stoned, Kate. I smelt it on your breath earlier."

"But Alfie . . ." Damn Charlie, bringing that whiskey. It's clear on Alfie's face, the redness in his cheeks, the way he averts his eyes from her. Why hadn't she noticed earlier, when everyone else knew he was drinking? "You made a promise to me, Aflie."

"Don't want to talk about it," Alfie snaps. "I'm fine. Leave me alone."

Kate paces to the far side of the helm deck and looks at the sea behind them. Maybe Alfie only had a shot or two. Perhaps he'll quit, won't touch another drop. She vowed to leave him if he drank again. After that last time, two years ago. He couldn't stop, hiding the bottles, taking a few hits before the morning coffee had brewed. Raving for more. She will not put up with that again.

A commotion breaks out on the deck below. Alfie stumbles out of the seat, gripping part of the helm for support.

"Alfie, the wheel!" Kate rushes towards him. "You forgot to secure it." He grabs hold before the wheel moves out of place. The vessel lurches as the sail stutters, as if to make up its mind whether to swing to the other side. An outcry bursts up from below. Alfie grabs the line from her and after a couple attempts manages to wrestle the loop onto a spoke of the wheel to keep it and the yacht steady. Alfie looks at her sheepishly as he stands with his hand on the headrest of the captain's seat. They stare at each other as they listen to the voices below.

On the main deck, Charlie and James yell at each other.

"Stop it!" Beatrice screams. "Alfie! Come down and help!"

Alfie pats the chair. "Take over here, Kate. Need to break them up."

"You're in no condition to do that, Alfie. Stay here."

"I'm the captain. No one gives me orders."

"You've had more than a shot or two, haven't you?" Kate looks at him, worried.

"Is it that obvious?" With a look of pained guilt, unsteady on his feet, Alfie staggers as the *Trinity* bounces at the wake of a larger vessel. His flailing arm grips the seat back at the third try.

"Sit down and steer the ship." Before you hurt yourself, Kate thinks to herself, let him stay at the wheel relaxed in the captain's chair until he sobered. Behind the wheel, Aflie gets a hold of himself, becoming calm in those times of turmoil. It's like a form of meditation for him, Kate thinks to herself as she rushes over to the ladder., and sees on the main deck below Charlie and James are swinging blows at each other and Beatrice stands to the side, yelling for them to stop.

Charlie hits James hard in the chin and James falls on the deck with a groan.

Kate scrambles down the ladder, and races across the deck where James lies on his side, clutching his face.

"Charlie! You hurt him! What has gotten into you?" Beatrice screams.

"He fucking deserved it." Charlie grabs Beatrice's arms and pushes her hard against the helm bulwark. "His bullshit and your bullshit. I'm sick of it." He lets go of her and storms away.

"He's gone crazy." In a state of shock, Beatrice plods towards James. "She's made him crazy."

Kate leans down. "James, are you okay?"

"I think so." He starts to pull himself up.

"You need to stay down, James," Kate says.

"See what I'm talking about, Kate?" Beatrice stands over her.

Kate looks up at her. "No, I don't, Beatrice."

"Charlie's woman. Look what she's done."

Kate glances around and doesn't see Evie. "She wasn't even here."

"But Charlie's behavior," Beatrice replies. "He's never acted this aggressively."

"That's what I'm trying to tell you, Beatrice," James groans. "That's why you can't believe a word he says."

"But you didn't have to start a fight, James." Beatrice scowls at James.

"Me?" James groans. "He attacked me. You saw everything."

"And what did he say about you and Evie?" Beatrice asks.

"Nothing!" James exclaims, blood dripping off his face.

Kate kneels at James' side. "You need to lie back. You've been injured."

29: James

"That racket! Listen to him rave! You see how he is." James tells Beatrice as they look up at the helm but Charlie and Alfie are out of sight beyond the steering console. "Like he's on meth or something."

"You think Charlie's on drugs?" Beatrice faces him, alarmed.

James smiles and sings to her: "Love is the drug and I need to score" while over her shoulder he sees Charlie at the ladder from the helm.

"James, this is no time to joke," Beatrice says quietly. "Do you really think Charlie's . . ."

"Charlie!" James says. Wary of his wife's reaction, but at least her attention is on Charlie, while Charlie has his eyes homed on James as he leaps from the ladder and stalks across the deck past the lounger chairs and Evie towards him and Beatrice. Evie sits there by herself, James thinks, waiting for someone to comfort her. Maybe while Beatrice and Charlie face off, James can walk past her and see if she wants to join him on the bow where they can resume their conversation.

"What was going on up there with you and Alfie?" Beatrice asks.

"Nothing." Charlie's face is tense, his lips glum, an expression James hasn't seen since that voyage decades earlier when Kate broke Charlie's heart. "It was nothing."

"It didn't sound like nothing, Charlie." Beatrice steps forward as James sinks slightly behind her.

"Don't blame me," Charlie replies. "He's shit-faced."

"Who's fault is that?" Beatrice is livid. "You bring that high-priced whiskey. You know Alfie has a weakness for it."

Charlie shrugs. "I thought this was a momentous occasion, to see off dear old dad. Not my fault he can't handle it." Beatrice flinches at Charlie's words, but Charlie hones past her and fixes on James, his look venomous. "Besides, James was the one who got him started."

"Me?" James laughs. "He's blaming me, Beatrice. So many lies, Charlie."

A look of shock is on Beatrice's face, half turned between James and Charlie as Charlie has stepped sideways and closer.

"Sure, James, like you wanted me to lie for you?" Charlie says.

"You really want to do that, Charlie?" James says as he gives Beatrice a comic roll of his eyes and clenches his cheeks for a what-the-fuck expression on his face. "Upset your sister with your stories?" He figures Charlie wants his sister to stay calm until they are off the ship, and now Charlie threatens to bring up that Evie was with them on Tuesday night? "Come to your senses, Charlie."

"It's not a story," Charlie says.

"Not a story? Don't listen to him."

"Why don't you tell her the lie, James." Charlie defiant, stands with his hands at his sides.

"James, what is Charlie talking about?" Beatrice asks.

"I have no idea. I don't know what's in Charlie's head."

"Look at you, stewing as you sweat in your lies, trying to stay calm," Charlie says.

Furious at Charlie, James' glibness melts. "Charlie, let's all agree to discuss this when we're back on shore."

Beatrice pushes past him to grasp Charlie's arm. "What're you talking about, Charlie?"

"He didn't want you to know about . . ." Charlie starts to say.

"Shut up, Charlie!" James clenches his fists. Charlie has no right to divulge a secret they made. He thought he could trust Charlie. And now Charlie wants to reveal the secret when they are isolated and confined on the *Trinity.*

"To know about what?" Beatrice asks Charlie while James steps to the other side of him." . . . the other evening. With me and Evie."

"That's a lie, Charlie! He's making . . ." James swallows. "Clearly he's delusional. Making stuff up, Beatrice."

Beatrice stares from Charlie to James. "She was there? James?" She steps closer to him. "I wondered, after what she told me."

"It's their word against mine," James says. "And you've always trusted me."

"She was there," Charlie says.

"James?" Beatrice narrows her eyes on him. "You said you and Charlie were alone."

"I forgot." James trembles nervously. "Maybe she came in when I left. I forgot about it."

Beatrice's face is contorted into an ugly frown that pulls her wrinkles into sharpness. "Are you sure, James? Where was she that night if they've been living together a month?"

"Who told you that?" James counters. "Charlie? Or her? You trust either of them?"

"Tell me the truth, James. Was that woman with you and Charlie that night?"

He doesn't have to say anything, she can see by the look on his face.

"Maybe. I don't remember. I didn't think it was important," James stammers.

"And today," Beatrice says. "You pretended you never met her before."

James scowls at Charlie before turning back to his wife. "Charlie's trying to cause problems, Beatrice. I don't remember her being there. You have to believe me."

"Maybe I should ask her" Beatrice points to Evie, on the deck a dozen feet beyond, clambering out of the lounge chair, her face fraught. "There she is, skulking about." Beatrice advances on Evie and Evie reels until her back is against the cabin bulwark.

"Beatrice, you can't trust her either!" James yells as he follows them.

"Get away from her, Beatrice!" Charlie demands and pushes in front of James.

But Beatrice seems not to hear as she stands in front of Evie "Tell me who's telling the truth."

Evie looks over at Charlie. "I was there. James is lying."

"Are you sure? You and Charlie aren't making things up?" Beatrice pushes her face close, her eyes inches from Evie's.

"Yes. James was there. And he . . ." Evie goes stiff with panic.

"Did you try to seduce him? Is that why he didn't want me to know?" Beatrice's face contorts with fury.

"No, he tried to . . ." Evie's eyes glisten wetly. But she doesn't finish, as if she can't decide whether to turn James in or seal their secrecy. At any moment Evie'll spill part of the story, James thinks, but in a way to implicate James and not herself. Make something up, re-interpret what happened between her and James to make him out a cad while downplaying her seduction of him, as if she's sweet and innocent and not a conniving hussy from the wrong side of the tracks.

Charlie and Evie teaming up against him. Both breaking promised secrets. James is furious. Charlie sneers at him, and Evie with her manufactured tears and her refusal to look at James. James feels his arms tremble with a need to move his fists as his hands clench tight. He'll slug that smirk off Charlie's face, he thinks helplessly.

"Tell me!" Beatrice grabs Evie by the shoulders. Evie stares at Beatrice in shock.

"Get your hands off her!" Charlie shoves Beatrice, his face raged red. Beatrice gasps.

"Hey! Don't!" James lights up in action. He shoves Beatrice out of the way as he leaps at Charlie, a fist swinging. Charlie blocks with an arm, and leaps back in a stance, his fists out too. The two men square off, six feet from each other in defensive crouches.

"You're a fucking liar, James!"

"James! Charlie! Stop it, you two!" Beatrice screams.

"Think you're tough, big boy. Come and get it!" James utters.

"I don't know why I felt sorry for you, you piece of shit." Charlie counters. James thinks he can take Charlie with a one-two. He steps in to do it but Charlie dodges the left fist and as James's right swing collides with Charlie's shoulder, Charlie's fist smacks James in the lower jaw with intense force. A flash of stars explodes in James' face as he belts out: "Oof!"

James feels the deck beneath his back and the sun in his face. He's not sure how he got there. Pain in his jaw and his shoulder and a dozen other places up and down his limbs. A blur of faces above him. Nice move, Charlie, James thinks. Win the fight but lose the battle. Beatrice will feel sorry for me, and she will realize how far gone you are. The bully and the martyr. The bully might have the upper hand now but the martyr wins in the end.

PART III: KNIVES AND GUNS

30: Charlie

Charlie stares down at James, lying on his back near his feet. What if I killed him? Charlie thinks with panic. No, the eyes are moving. James clutches his jaw and groans with pain. Charlie steps away, fear and anger replaced with contriteness at hurting James, but also a sense of moral superiority. James had it coming to him.

Charlie's hand throbs with pain, and he rubs the knuckles to massage the pain away. He looks over at Kate and Beatrice. They both stare back at him as if they have no idea who he is.

"How could you?" Kate scolds as she rushes past Charlie to kneel next to James.

"Charlie?" Beatrice has a stunned look on her face.

"Charlie!" Alfie barks from the helm. "Come here!"

"Charlie, what got into you?" Beatrice makes a wide fearful path around him to reach James, lying on the deck. Blood dribbles down the side of James' face.

"He swung first," Charlie says. "He deserved it." He glances around. Where is Evie, to defend him? Beatrice and Kate kneel at James' prone body. "You all saw it," Charlie says. "He swung first." Kate glances up at him with a scowl.

"Charlie! Up here now!" Alfie's voice is hoarse and furious, reminding Charlie of their father, yelling commands like they were all in the fucking navy.

Beatrice looks up, her face grim. "You'd better get up there, Charlie."

"Yeah? I will. Get off my fucking case," Charlie mutters. He walks slowly to the ladder to the helm. A mix of emotions rushes through him as he ascends, fear of discipline and the bitterness he feels towards his family.

The captain's chair turned towards the ladder, Alfie watches Charlie climb to the deck. Charlie stares at him, almost forgetting he's looking at his brother and not his father in earlier days. Alfie wears the same naval cap, and his jowls are locked in the same condemnation.

"I think you owe me an apology," Alfie says, a smug grin pushing away the grimace.

"You?" Charlie shakes his head. "I might owe James one. Stupid of me." He starts to rub his knuckles again.

"Now you know it's true, don't you?"

"Know what's true?"

"About James and Evie." Alfie lets out a gust of laughter. "That's why you decked him"

"I decked him because he threw a punch first," Charlie says.

"You and James were fighting over her. What else would make you two go at it like that?"

Again with the accusations. Charlie's anger flares. "What are you talking about, you drunk old man?"

"Don't talk to me like that!" Alfie stumbles out of the seat to face Charlie. Though heavier than Charlie, he's less steady on his feet. The fear Charlie once felt with Alfie or their father is no longer there.

"I'll talk to you how I want," Charlie says. "What will you do about it, old fool?"

Alfie flinches and reels back a half step, as if Charlie's words dealt a physical blow. Fear flashes across Alfie's face before he steals himself. Alfie pumps out his chest, his arms at his sides, and his unbuttoned shirt flaps back to reveal the handle of the revolver. "You want to change your tune, little brother?"

"Seriously? You're going to threaten me with your gun?" Charlie laughs bitterly. "I'm not afraid of you." Without thinking about it, Charlie has taken a step back. The confidence flows out of him at the sight of the gun, though he knows Alfie has it on him. Alfie wouldn't use it, would he? But with

Alfie's inebriation . . . Charlie is not certain. Charlie's own drunkenness, he's not as scared as he thinks he should be.

"I've made a decision," Alfie says. "We stop at Port Angeles. She's off the *Trinity*."

"You can't do that."

"I'm the captain. Beatrice and James are right. Look at the trouble she's caused."

"James and Beatrice caused the trouble. Kick them off."

"I've made up my mind, Charlie. She can't be on the yacht."

"But.. but.. I'm getting off too. I don't give a fuck about Dad's ashes or the rest of you."

"You'd do that?" Alfie looks surprised. "You'd lose some inheritance."

"What kind of narcissistic asshole puts in his will that you get less money if you fail to see his ashes get scattered? I don't fucking care about that," Charlie growls.

"Don't talk about Dad like that. Dad wanted the best for you, Charlie. You never saw him in the hospital when he got ill. It hurt him, the way you threw your life away. Your weaknesses."

"Spare me the bullshit, Alfie." Past his brother's shoulder, Charlie notices Evie at the bow. He steps around Alfie to the edge of the steering console to get a better look. She has her back to them. What is she doing up there by herself? She was about to say something before Beatrice pushed her against the bulwark. Something about James. Now she is at the front of the yacht, avoiding Charlie.

Charlie pulls out the flask, now filled with the other single-malt, and takes a swig as he keeps his eyes on Evie. He gets a tap on his shoulder as he stares. He holds up the flask and Alfie grabs it.

Alfie's insinuations about James whisper in Charlie's thoughts as he remembers the night he and Evie spent with James . . . that night after James left and the next morning, Evie was quiet and secretive, and at the time he didn't pay much attention, shrugged it off as a hangover, but now he begins to wonder. What was Evie keeping from him that night? And why?

"Take the wheel, Charlie," Alfie says behind him. "I think there's a vessel out there."

Charlie sees it too, beyond the bow, at the port side, a much larger motor yacht nearing the *Trinity*. "Sure thing, Alfie," he mutters. He sits down behind the wheel, though the other vessel's trajectory is well beyond theirs. At the front of the *Trinity*, Evie turns to follow the other yacht's progress, her body in half profile. Laughter and yells and the sounds of disco carry across the water. A large banner on the front of the hull proclaims a wedding celebration. On the decks are several men and women, twenty-and-thirty-somethings, tanned bodies, solid abs and pecs shiny with oil.

Alfie hands back the flask and Charlie pockets it.

"Just what we fucking need," Charlie remarks. "Those assholes and their wake."

"Yeah." Alfie cracks a smile as the line of white in the water moves closer. "Fucking lubbers, think they're in a damn beer commercial. Dad would snarl at them."

"Yuppie scum," Charlie says. "Dad'd whip out his gun just to throw the scare in them."

"That's the spirit, Charlie." Alfie smiles.

The *Trinity* gets tossed as the wake shoves past them. The other yacht is behind them. Evie following it now looks towards Charlie. He waves his hand. At that distance her face is inscrutable. She puts her hands out to her sides. He beckons her with his hand. Does she look slightly ashen? She trudges slowly towards the side deck. Why is she afraid or hesitant to confront him? Suspicion crawls into his head. He glances over his shoulder to see Alfie is still on the helm, urinating off the rear.

"Hey, Alfie?"

"What do you want?" Alfie grunts.

"I want to know what you saw in the cabin," Charlie says.

Alfie zips up and turns to face him. "Decided to save a trip. You want to make something of it?"

"Did you really see them in the cabin? James and Evie?"

31: Evie

Alone on the bow, slumped against the cabin wall, Evie takes deep breaths, letting the briny air fill her lungs before letting it out again. Her mind still reels, the eruption of violence, cascading into more violence, Beatrice attacking her, Charlie pushing Beatrice, James hitting Charlie. Charlie's face contorted and red and unrecognizable as he puts up his fists to fight James. Hurling challenges at each other. She couldn't deal with the panic, couldn't even call out, yell at them to stop. In terror she escaped, barely aware as she scrambled across the narrow side walkway to the front of the boat, where the angry voices were dampened by the wind and the crackle of the jib sail.

Will Charlie think she deserted him? He brought her with him because he wanted her help in dealing with them. Evie should have rushed in and tried to break him and James up. Why didn't anyone do anything?

Why didn't he tell her his family is so crazy? Or did he, and she hadn't listen? Eccentric is what she was thinking, not full-blown head-cases. What she imagined would be a pleasant pleasure cruise becomes increasingly more a nightmare. Maybe she should get off at Port Angeles, though Charlie doesn't want her to. She stands at the front tip of the yacht, holding on to the rope railing, looking at the sea ahead as if there's any clue of an approaching port.

Another ship heads towards them. The yacht is larger than the *Trinity* and with no sails. It moves at a clip to the left of them. Evie wipes the wet from her eyes and peers out at them. The other ship has the sounds of a wedding party, the bubble of mirth and yelling and conversation over the beats of electronic dance music. A couple of empty champagne bottles fly in an arch overboard.

Several men and women wave to her, others raise glasses in a toast, and she limply waves back, and imagines what it would be like to be on that boat instead, having a good time. Or would she, alone among these young athletic party-goers? Anything would be better than the drama aboard the *Trinity*. To see these people enjoy themselves, she wants to feel that joy too. Let it push past the turmoil in her

head, the fear, the sadness. She waves and smiles. A chorus of "whoos!" wells up from the other ship, Dionysian banshees.

Seventy yards away, the yacht passes the *Trinity*. The voices and the music, all but the thump thump of the bass, barely make it over the wash of the waves. She turns to follow their progress. As they get further behind, Evie notices Charlie at the helm behind the wheel. She's relieved he's not hurt from the fight with James. Alfie is on the deck behind him. With a flip of his hand, Charlie beckons her.

Evie has trepidation. She pushes back that image of Charlie red with anger, facing off with James for arm-to-arm combat with bare, hard fists. Temporary insanity takes over Charlie's face and hands. And James, just as furious, the vein reddened in the side of his head. To hurl at each other with knuckles in primal combat trying to smack the other down, like cavemen.

She reaches the side deck and squints to see Charlie more clearly. His back now is to her, as he talks to Alfie. Half hidden behind Charlie's back, Alfie has a grin.

Maybe Alfie can help her tell Charlie about what happened in the cabin. Alfie must have seen how frightened she was while James was swallowed by guilt, his face beat red. She wants to thank Alfie for stopping James.

Evie's more confident on the narrow side deck, this her fifth or sixth time. She reaches the main deck. The others are huddled at the far side from where she climbs down. She hopes to get to the ladder to the steering area without anyone seeing her. Luckily Beatrice's back is to her while Kate faces her, both women kneeling. But why, in between them, is James flat on the ground? Did Charlie hurt him?

She steps quietly, slowly across the deck. Kate and Beatrice converse in low tones, words indecipherable to Evie as she inches across the deck. Kate glances up and sees her over Beatrice's shoulder.

"Go on, Kate," Beatrice says. Beatrice turns to follow Kate's gaze and flinches at the sight of Evie. "Evie. Where've you been hiding?"

"I'm . . . I didn't want any of this to happen," Evie blurts.

"But it did happen. James has been injured."

"It's not all her fault," Kate says.

"I'm sorry." Evie pulls away from the cursing eyes and continues towards the ladder to the helm.

Why am I sorry? Evie thinks. Why did they blame her for James and Charlie's behavior? Even Kate, saying "not all" instead of "none" or "hardly none," still heaving most of the guilt on Evie, while Beatrice would out-right blame her if the *Trinity* hit an ice burg.

As she thinks that, Evie has a premonition of an ice burg lying beneath, or a storm raging up above. A ship is sinking . . . survivors swimming or in a dinky dinghy. To sink as fish food or to wash up on some far off shore, a remote magical island like in *The Tempest*, or a place where she disguises herself as a man and falls in love with a duke on a *Twelfth Night*.

Evie scales the ladder to the steering console. His back to her, Alfie talks in a hushed tone. " . . . type of woman she is.. loose morals . . .Promise you anything. Not the first time you've been blindsided." Charlie sees her but doesn't acknowledge her while Alfie rattles on. She waits for Charlie to defend her, but Charlie twists his mouth to give his whole face a petulant ugliness. Alfie turns to face her as well.

"What's wrong?" Evie asks.

32: Beatrice

"I can't take any more of this," Beatrice tells Kate. "You might think she's innocent but . . ."

Poor James on the deck in front of her, his face bloodied. Charlie carrying on like a madman. Alfie drunk. And Kate, unwilling to admit something is terribly wrong.

Beatrice stands, slightly dizzy. Flashes of red flit at the edges of her vision, and she feels a storm cloud in the back of her head. "I think I need to take something."

"You should, Beatrice," Kate nods.

The meds will suppress the anger, dull the far-off pile-driver pound-ing. Beatrice staggers down the steps to the cabin. She bends down to cra-dle her father's urn. His image in the glazed surface looks up at her. What would Farley do in this situation? Would he let it get this far? Why can't he be here to bring order, to reign in the unraveling chaos?

Beatrice goes to her carry-on, and reaches into the side pocket for the pills. That's odd. The blister pack is not tucked way down the way she left it. As she pulls it out, a coldness grips her. Two of the pills are missing.

There's only one suspect. Evie! A drug addict and a thief! Now Be-atrice has only two pills and not four. She stuffs the remaining two back into the bag and storms back up to the main deck to confront Evie. In her rush of anger, she realizes she forgot to take one of the pills . . . she will probably need both, she realizes, in her panic, and then she won't have any, which will make her panic more.

But Beatrice first needs to tell Kate. Surely this will convince Kate.

"Kate," she says as she crosses the deck.

"What is it?" Kate looks up from James.

"She stole my meds!"

"Stole your meds? Why would she . . .? Are you sure?"

"Of course I'm sure."

"You didn't misplace them?" Kate asks.

"Why are you doubting my words?" Beatrice prickles as she glares at Kate. "She stole my meds."

"I'm not doubting you, Beatrice. I just think . . ." Kate goes quiet at the sound of angry voices from the helm.

"Why is everything going crazy?" Beatrice gets on one knee to get close to James. "And James, putting himself in the middle of it. Poor James."

"He should be fine, Beatrice."

Beatrice glances up. Her voice is quiet. "Why did he lie to me?"

"Take some deep breaths, Beatrice, and wait for the meds to kick in."

"The meds?" Beatrice'd forgotten to take them, but she'll go down after she talks to James.

James' eyes flutter. He's awake.

"James?" she asks. "Can you hear me?"

He moans.

Beatrice crouches down, her face inches from his. "What's going on James?"

"Maybe you should wait, Beatrice," Kate says.

A loud thump from the back shakes the deck. "What was that?" Beatrice asks. She glances up to see Kate leaving to check it out. Beatrice bends closer. "James? Can you hear me?"

Another moan.

"James, you need to tell me what Alfie saw."

"Ask Alfie," James moans. "He'll tell you everything. I didn't do anything."

"But you lied to me. About her being at Charlie's."

"It's not my fault. Talk to Alfie. He'll tell you what kind of woman she is. Talk to Alfie."

"Maybe I will." She glances up. What's going on across the deck near the helm? Alarmed she gets to her feet.

33: James

James lies on the deck, his face in pain. How did he let Charlie get that punch in? He didn't think Charlie had it in him, and Charlie took him by surprise. Even Charlie had a surprised look on his face as his head floated away and James fell backward to the deck.

Now Beatrice hovers over him. At least she's not interrogating him about Charlie's accusation. At least Kate convinces Beatrice to take a pill. The chill pills are what she called her meds. To chill her out. Beatrice agrees she should take one and now he's alone on the deck with Kate. He looks up at her. Kate, the same age as him. Why didn't he end up with Kate instead of Beatrice?

"He knocked you pretty good there, James," Kate says.

"Didn't think he was so tough," he says. "Didn't see it in him like you do."

"You guys can't do this shit. Not out here. No hospitals nearby."

"You're a nurse. You can nurse me back to health any time, Kate." He imagines having a three-way with her and Evie. At first he thought she was jealous of Charlie and Evie, but now . . . Her and Evie have a certain intimacy when they're together. Charlie the libertine. He realizes he envies Charlie, having sex with Kate and with Evie. It's not right, Charlie is such a putz otherwise. He, James should be the one.

Kate looks away from him. Someone approaches from the cabin. "Beatrice?" she calls out.

"Kate! She stole my meds!"

"Why would she do that?" Kate asks.

Because she's a drug addict? James wants to say. Will even do drugs when she doesn't know what they are?

"I don't know. But they're gone." Beatrice says.

James shuts his eyes. Did Evie really steal the rest of Beatrice's pills? It would be just the sort of move to totally fuck things up. James still has one pill in his pocket, but he can't say anything about it. He doesn't want Beatrice's wrath directed at him. Not when she hasn't taken one yet.

Eyes shut, he senses darkness as Beatrice hovers over him, blocking the sun. "James, can you hear me?" Beatrice says.

He moans, as if in pain. I'm suffering right now. Go away and leave me alone. But no, she has her face in his, asking him about something Alfie said. He tells her to talk to Alfie. Anything to get her out of his face so he can think of his next move. He has never hated her as much as he hates her now.

34: Charlie

The motor yacht has become a dot behind them. Charlie gets out of the captain's seat and faces his brother Alfie. Their anger at each other has subsided.

"What's that?" Alfie steps closer.

"James and Evie. You really see them together in the cabin?"

"That's what I told you, Charlie."

"What were they doing?"

"I don't know. Conspiring. Caught in the act. Suspicious as hell."

"What do you mean? Were they . . .How close.. Like.."

"In each other's arms?" Alfie nods. "I think so. They backed away from each other when they heard me."

"Are you sure?" Charlie stares at his brother.

"Guilty looks, both of them," Alfie says. "When I came out of the can, she'd fled, and James pretended it was nothing, tried to convince me . . ."

"You're not making shit up?"

"I'm not a liar, Charlie. Some of us abide to moral principals, believe in Jesus and God . . .."

"You saw them making out? Kissing?"

"I think so." Alfie nods.

"What do you mean, you think so?"

"They stopped when they heard me. They were backing away from each other." Alfie rubs the top of his head as if to massage memory into it as he re-tilts the admiral's cap. "Before that, they were . . . in each other's arms I think."

"You think? What did you see?"

"I wasn't paying attention when I came down the steps. They were at the far end of the cabin. It was clear they were up to something, the way they were acting, all nervous as if caught in the act."

Charlie glowers at Alfie. "Maybe you just think you saw something, you drunk old fool." Beyond Alfie, Evie's head appears at the ladder to the main deck.

Alfie, unaware she's on the deck, continues: "Don't get pissed at me, Charlie. Everyone can see what type of woman she is. Loose morals, promiscuity. Not the first time you've been blindsided."

Evie steps onto the deck. "What's going on, Charlie?"

"You want to tell me?"

"I'm glad you're not hurt. I couldn't deal with it. You and James fighting." Her face is wet with tears. Her words, nervously spoken with hesitation.

"Didn't want to take sides?" he asks.

"I was afraid," she says. "Is there something wrong, Charlie?"

"Alfie tells me he caught you and James making out in the cabin."

Evie's lower jaw drops in shock. "No! That's not it at all."

"Are you calling me a liar?" Alfie spews.

"He was trying to . . ." She chokes on the words.

"He was what?" Charlie steps closer to her. "Don't lie to me."

"He attacked me."

"Attacked you? James?"

"Not what it looked like to me," Alfie chimes in.

"He attacked me, Charlie."

"Why didn't you tell me?" Charlie asks.

"I . . . I was going to tell you," Evie replies.

"She's putting all the blame on James," Alfie says. "How can you believe her?"

"Shut the fuck up, you drunk old man!" Charlie snaps back as he peers into Evie's face, trying to ascertain the truth behind her tears and fearful look."You didn't tell me, Evie."

"He did it at the condo too," she says. "When you were crashed out at the table. He tried to get fresh with me."

"You didn't say anything about it."

"I wanted to forget it happened. Just some drunk stupid thing he didn't mean to do and that he'd learned his lesson."

"Are you lying to me?" He grips her shoulders.

"Please, Charlie. Get your arms off of me. I'm telling the truth."

"Why didn't you tell me earlier?" Charlie demands.

"I . . . I don't know," Evie sobs. "Charlie please . . ."

Charlie releases her. He doesn't know if he believes her and that doubt overwhelms him, a powerful wave that rises and threatens to crash down until he starts falling inside his head even as he's aware he's still on his feet on the helm deck with her and Alfie, the precise feeling he had twenty-two years earlier, in the same location when Kate wearing the same bikini told him it was over, with Alfie behind her to back her up.

No! This can't happen again! Evie reels away from him. Alfie stares at him with smug superiority, the same smugness as his father. He can't remember if it is Alfie or his father on the deck that day over two decades ago, Alfie the same age now their father was then, that day Kate shattered his heart into a million pieces. It was like they were all in on it and Charlie is last to know he'd been betrayed on the worst day of his life.

Dizzy, Charlie's vision blurs, the blurred shape in the bikini, Kate when her hair was long, and Alfie or their father, standing behind her. The terrible claws of jealousy gnaw into his chest. A chasm looms at the back of his mind, an eddy that threatens to suck him deep into bleak misery. He wanted to hit Alfie, pummel him with his fists, but he was too afraid, his brother bigger and more muscular, hardened by Naval training, and instead Charlie sunk deeper into the morass of futility.

"No!" Charlie steels himself to fight the downward pull. He won't be a victim again, he will pull himself back up as he sucks in a deep breath and clenches his whole body as if to squeeze out the memory of despair. His vision sharpens. He focuses on Alfie, who looks back at him with a contemptuous sneer.

"Accept the truth, Charlie. Don't have a sissy fit. Like that other time."

Alfie and their father, same rigid cruelty, the same smug superiority, unwilling to admit error. The rage explodes inside Charlie.

"Fuck you, Alfie!" Charlie lunges at him. Alfie, startled, throws up his arms in defense and reels back, almost loses his footing as his face bursts with panic. Alfie staggers upright and crouches forward, hands in front of him. "You think you can take me, you little shit."

"Shut up, you drunk old fart. I'm not afraid of you." Charlie's confidence is boosted by Alfie's moment of panic. Charlie takes another step forward.

"You shut the fuck up! Stop acting crazy Charlie." Alfie straightens his back. The outline of the gun's handle is clear beneath the shirt. Alfie has his hands at his sides, like a gunslinger ready to reach and draw.

"I'm not afraid of you," Charlie says. "What are you going to do? Shoot me? Would you dare?"

"What's gotten into you?" Alfie takes another step back, to keep a distance between them. Behind Alfie is the ladder down to the main deck, the only section of the helm with no railing. Alfie's foot lands half off the deck, and he loses his footing, and his balance. Scrabbling to catch hold, a look of shock stretching his face, he falls and vanishes to the deck below with a loud thunk and a groan.

"Charlie! What have you done?" Evie rushes over. Charlie steps slowly to the edge, out of breath and scared. On the deck below, Alfie lies sprawled on his side.

35: Kate

Beatrice looks up from James. "What was that?"

"That sound?" Kate heard it too, a loud thump that shook the deck. She can't see Aflie or Charlie on the helm from her angle. She yells out: "Alfie?" She stands and steps around Beatrice and James. She sees the shape at the bottom of the ladder to the helm. "Alfie?" He's on his hands and knees, trying to get to his feet. She stumbles closer. Up above Evie and Charlie look down.

"What the fuck?" Kate says. "Charlie? Evie?"

"Is Alfie okay?" Evie staggers down the ladder.

"I don't know." Kate leans over him. "Alfie?"

Alfie dazed doesn't hear her, as he groans and tries to sit up.

"Alfie? Stop that. You might injure something."

"I'll injure that fucking brother of mine is what I'll do. Help me to my feet, Kate."

"No, Alfie! You need to lie down and relax."

"Not when he's up there pretending to run the ship."

Evie approaches, slowly and tentatively. "Is Alfie okay?"

"I don't know," Kate says. "What the fuck was going on up there?"

"They got in a fight," Evie says. "Alfie backed too far, fell off."

"That's a lie!" Alfie grunts. "He pushed me! Caught me by surprise, the scoundrel."

"Alfie, please."

"I don't need anyone's help," he mutters.

Kate glances around and points. "Evie, bring that lounge chair here."

Evie stumbles across the deck, and returns pulling the chair behind her. Charlie has joined them, standing several feet away, at the rail near the helm bulwark. He looks pale, Kate thinks as she glances up at him. "I need help getting him in the lounger." She waves over Charlie. "We need to get him into the chair. Evie, you hold it in place."

"What are you doing?" Alfie asks as Kate grabs his shoulders and Charlie his lower torso. They push him up to the lounge chair, the back down flat. Alfie grunts loudly as he falls and the chair groans beneath him.

"There. Isn't that more comfortable?" Kate asks.

"I can't lie around. I need to run the ship."

"Take a brief rest, Alfie. Hope you didn't break anything."

Crouched at James' side, Beatrice turns and sees them. Alarmed, she rises to her feet. "What's wrong with Alfie?" She storms across the deck. "Poor Alfie."

"He fell," Evie says.

"Fell? Or maybe you pushed him?" Beatrice snarls back.

"That's right. Charlie must of pushed me!" Alfie tries to sit up, but Kate holds him down with her hand on his chest.

"Charlie's crazy!" Beatrice rants.

"Me?" Charlie wails. "It's his fault!"

Kate tunes out the angry voices as she runs her fingers down the ribs beneath Alfie's shirt. He seemed to have trouble focusing on her as if he's going in and out of consciousness, but now he looks at her with misty eyes. "Kate?"

She bends closer to his face. "You're going to be okay, Alfie. You need to relax."

"You're not pissed off at me for drinking?"

"I'm very pissed off. But I don't want you hurt, Alfie."

"The triangle bikini. Were you in it today?" he asks.

"The bikini?" Kate shakes her head. "No. Just this one."

"I was thinking about you in it. Remember that day?"

"That was a long time ago, Alfie. Why are you bringing this up?" Is the blow to his head making him think weird things? And Charlie, seven yards away, though Alfie's voice is so low she doesn't think Charlie can hear him.

Alfie smiles as if he's unaware he has just fallen from the higher deck. "You and that bathing suit. And free of Charlie. That's when we let him know it was serious."

"I don't like to think about that, Alfie."

"I feel like he's getting revenge for that time. Charlie and that wench in your old bikini. Why did you let her wear it?"

"I told you. Only one that fit her."

"I don't trust Charlie. Keep an eye on him. In case I fall asleep or something. If I do, take this." Alfie pats the side of his gut. His hand trembles and searches, the empty holster, fingers splayed and wiggling like four serpents, and the thumb dragging like a slug. He trembles with alarm. "Whah? Where is my . . .?"

36: James

Lying on his back on the deck, James is relieved the others are not around him. Their voices from the other side of the main deck are unintelligible over the ocean and the sails. He thinks he could close his eyes and fall asleep. Then he hears Alfie bellow.

"The gun! Where's my gun?"

"There it is! She has it." Beatrice, shrill and desperate, the manic craze taking over her voice. "She can't have it! You! Don't pick up that gun!"

James cringes. Beatrice with the gun? He was at the end of his rope. She now thought he was guilty, even as he told her how sorry and weak he was. He told her what happened. Evie kept throwing herself at him because Charlie wasn't enough for her, and he kept pushing Evie away. He told Beatrice he felt bad for Charlie, how Charlie blithely laughed it off while hurt inside, Charlie's heart poisoned by this seductress. He, James, fought valiantly to keep his virtue, and for Charlie's sake, he didn't want to blab Charlie's embarrassment.

Of course, Beatrice didn't believe it. As she knelt over him, her eyes peering into his, her face twisted into ugly despair. She was angry and suspicious. Even if nothing happened and he told her nothing happened, she would think the worst, that he desired the woman. He does not think he can lie about that. He does want Evie. Ever since that night. He couldn't stop thinking about her these past several days. Lying beside Beatrice at night with the image of Evie in his head, until he snuck into the bathroom to rub one off. Seeking porn clips on his phone for girls with Evie's slim shape and pixie face and long wavy black hair.

But now Beatrice was on the other side of the main deck. Just having her out of his face took the edge off. James rubs his legs. Twisting sideways, intensifying the throb in his shoulder where he hit the deck, equal to the duller one in his jaw.

James sees some of the others at the far side of the deck, kneeling over someone. Maybe Alfie threw Charlie off the helm, James wonders, wishing he hadn't missed the look on Charlie's face. Maybe one of them fell off drunk. And where is Evie? He refuses to worry another look. Maybe she's alone in the cabin. Or at the bow? Had he seen her head that way when he and Charlie faced off? Maybe she thought Charlie would get hurt, wuss that he was. It was about time James gave Charlie a throttling to show who is real and who is bullshit.

The reverie dissolves when he hears Alfie moan for his missing gun. Why the fuck did Alfie have to bring that fucking thing in the first place? And then gets shitfaced while carrying it around? And now Alfie doesn't have it?

"You! Don't dare pick up that gun!" Beatrice's voice pierces the air.

A mewling sob he doesn't recognize, too low to make out many words. "I.. I.. pick it up!"

"No! I pick up the gun!" Beatrice's voice is shrill. Fuck! Just what we need, Beatrice in one of her fits with a gun. Lashed with fear, James crawls to the gear locker at the other side of the helm bulkhead, out of sight of the others. He pulls off the padlock and opens the door. The single spear gun, loaded with the one harpoon, hangs on the wall, while the line that attaches them falls coiled at the bottom. Alfie had loaded it earlier, and reaching for it now sends a shiver down James's back.

What is James thinking? The harpoon idea scares him as he looks down at the weapon. Taking it out would probably get him shot if Beatrice has Alfie's gun. What if he accidentally triggered it, like Charlie did that time? He stumbles away from the cabinet, leaving the door open and the harpoon gun exposed. Still panicking about Beatrice on the far side of the vessel with the gun, James crawls across the deck towards the cabin. Still dizzy from the blow. Get down below, before they see him. He almost stumbles down the steps to the interior of the yacht.

Let Beatrice have the gun. What is there to lose? As long as he's nowhere near looking into the barrel. Maybe the best thing that could happen, Beatrice, angry and armed, ready to blow up at Alfie for being drunk and Charlie and Evie. Most likely Evie, James thinks with remorse. He'll help Charlie convict Beatrice, and then he and Charlie can make up for this stupid day.

Maybe Beatrice will shoot Charlie. Charlie beating his older brother to a pulp, the way he tried with James, like an insane animal. Beatrice must realize what a jar of explosives her brother is and he probably scares her. If Charlie dies, sad, but James and Evie commiserate their loss together while Beatrice gets hauled off to jail or the psych ward. Makes perfect sense. Almost ideal, one might say, not that James would say it.

She could kill any of them once she starts waving the gun around feeling her power over them. But if Evie went to the bow, like he saw, then . . .

Maybe Kate? Beatrice is upset at Kate as well, for possibly sleeping with Charlie two years ago. No one knows if they had other trysts. Maybe Kate is responsible for the fistfight between Charlie and Alfie, watch them slug it out to decide if she made the wrong choice twenty-odd years ago. Kate acting so sweet, but really there's something dark and sneaky inside her. It would kill Alfie to be beaten up by Charlie. Maybe Charlie crippled him, to leave him wheelchair-bound and helpless while she could cheat with Charlie even more. If it's Kate, that's sad, but not the worst thing that could happen.

Maybe Beatrice'll kill herself. A couple times she threatened to do that. Sobbing one moment, screaming the next on a manic roller coaster.

She cut her hand with a knife once, but she blamed it on him, and he's not sure if it was an accident.

But a gun is far more lethal than a knife. All it would take is one split moment where she has that gun in her hand, and the suicidal impulse pops into her head and out again, or maybe not when in less than a second she could blow her brains out? Or would she first make a speech. "I'm going to blow my brains." Regardless, it would be a trip to the morgue and not the hospital for stitches.

James would feel really bad if that happened, because he did love Beatrice enough not to want to have her seriously hurt, just put in a place to keep her and everyone safe. She was mostly unhappy to begin with, the more she showed her age, and sometimes people want to go somewhere else and they can't think of any other way to get there. It would be terrible if Beatrice took her own life, and he'd feel bad, but how terrible should he feel? It would be a burden completely off his back and not her withering in a cell as a murderer and getting out and later coming back to him accusingly. And as a widower, her inheritance would be his, unlike a divorcee.

A lot of ways this could go, he thinks to himself as he glances around the cabin. He needs to stop his head from racing. He almost has the crazy thought of masturbating to Evie's image and spunking in Farley's urn to take his anger out on all of them. Instead he has another swag of whiskey to calm his nerves. He also pulls the longest knife out of the kitchen drawer and hides it beneath his towel at the corner of the table. Just in case he needs to defend himself. He peers out the forward hatch, no one there.

He's in too much pain to keep moving, He sits down in a chair, flops his face on the table and the pain eases. Charlie hit him pretty hard, how did he think Charlie wouldn't hit him that hard? After ten minutes rest, he rises to his feet again. He stumbles to the back portal puts his ear to the doorway. Their voices carry across the deck. He can't tell who has the gun. Beatrice's shrill voice is the clearest, but the others are angry too, one voice on top of another, no one finishing with everyone interrupting and it all too faint to make out words. He shambles into the berth and sinks down on the bed. He no longer hears the voices. He'll rest until he hears the gun go off. Though exhausted, his mind races too quickly for sleep, keeping him in an intermediate zone between awake and slumber. He listens to the lap of the waves and the creaks of the vessel and other far-off sounds. It seems as if things have calmed down.

He hears the gun. A shot, and then a moment later, three more.

37: Evie

Evie is petrified as she stands on the main deck. In front of her, Beatrice is livid. "Charlie's gone crazy! It's her that's done it to him!" Beatrice points to Evie. Evie shrinks back two steps until her foot hits something hard. She looks down. Alfie's gun. Lying on the deck, and pointed towards Charlie, who stands at the rail seven or eight feet from the other, observing them.

"It's his fault," Charlie says. "He threatened me with his gun. He used to beat me up when I was a kid. Now the shoe's on the other foot, and if he gives me any lip, that shoe's going right up his ass."

"Where is the gun, Alfie? Where did you lose it?" Grasping the front of his shirt, Kate shakes Alfie.

"Don't let him have it!" Charlie belts. "Not if he's threatening people with it."

"We can't have a lost gun on deck. For God's sake, Alfie," Beatrice wails.

The gun scares Evie. She's too scared to reach down and touch it, even as she bends down for a closer look. She almost thinks the gun's an hallucination, the others not noticing it on the deck at her feet, shiny in the sunlight with chrome curves and ornate work on the wooden handle, an object of minimalist beauty, this dangerous weapon.

"There it is! She has it!" Beatrice points to Evie. "Stop her! She can't pick it up!"

"I don't want it," Evie stutters.

"Don't let her have it, Evie!" Charlie's voice penetrates the others to her ear. Beatrice storms at her like an angry boar and dives for the gun. Evie takes a half step back. Fingers curl around the handle as Evie kicks at it. The forward swing of her foot collides with Beatrice's hand and the gun.

Beatrice shrieks loudly. The gun glides across the deck to an opening in the railing. The gun teeters at the edge. Beatrice lunges again and the vessel lurches and the gun teeters again and falls. Evie watches it vanish with relief, its lethal presence a danger, and now it's gone, falling slowly to the bottom of the sea. One can barely hear the splash over the lurching of the mast, the gasps from Beatrice, and the slap of the waves on the hull.

"What have you done? We don't have a gun? What if we are attacked by pirates?" Beatrice rails.

"Seriously Beatrice, we're safer without it," Kate replies.

"That was Dad's favorite gun! And she kicks it into the sea? As if she hasn't been cruel enough to Alfie." Beatrice advances on Evie. Evie begins to back away.

"That's not right," Evie gasps. "I had nothing to do with this."

"Then why are you trying to evade me. Why can't you face me? You stole my drugs and now this. You're so full of guilt."

"I'm scared of you, but that doesn't mean I'm guilty!" Evie says, but her words are lost to louder voices.

"Fuck you, Beatrice! Get the fuck away from her!" Charlie stomps loudly across the deck.

"Beatrice! You need to calm down!" Kate slowly moves closer.

Beatrice will have none of it. "Why doesn't anyone see what's happening? Why is everyone taking her side? She stole my meds!"

A hand smacks Evie's face. Sparks flash in her head at impact. She keeps on her feet and feels the sting on her cheek. In front of her, Beatrice cocks her hand back. Evie shuts her eyes and waits for another blow. She doesn't know what else to do, and she thinks if she prepares for it, it won't startle as much, and she will get used to the pain.

Loud noises around her, but trailing off. She opens her eyes. The others are at the far side of the deck, except for Alfie who lies eight feet away from her in a lounge chair. He lumbers slowly to his feet and when he spots her he locks eyes with her. He seems to be in a dream as he stares at her.

"Kate! There you are! I just had the most frightful nightmare."

"Alfie, that's not me." Evie shakes her head.

"You think Charlie wants revenge? For stealing you from him?" Alfie sways unsteady on his feet. His eyes don't quite focus right.

"Alfie, I'm not Kate. Maybe you should lie back down." Evie steps closer to him.

"Yes. Alfie and Kate. Come here, Kate. You think Charlie would hear us if we made love on the bow? He certainly hasn't taken it very well, losing you."

"Not Kate!" she says more loudly, unsure if Alfie hears her. He stumbles towards her. The vessel lurches and he staggers back toward the rail. "Be careful, Alfie!"

He stumbles and tips backward, across the railing. She rushes towards him. The yacht lurches again and his upper torso is flung into the space beyond the railing. His hands claw the air as he goes over backward. A surprised look on his face is the last thing she sees for the second time him falling off a deck, but this time into the sea.

A shrill voice stabs into her:

"She's killed him! Pushed him off the deck! Murder!"

38: Beatrice

The foot slams pain in Beatrice's hand. The gun escapes her grasp, to skitter across the deck to the edge. On all fours, she scuttles towards it. Almost has her fingers on the handle when it slides off the edge as if Evie used telekinesis to will it out of Beatrice's grasp.

On her hands and knees, and with no gun, Beatrice feels humiliated. To be reduced to an animal. She looks over her shoulder. The others stare at her as they stand fanned out on the deck behind her, Charlie, Kate, and Evie. Evie is several feet in front of the other two as if to show Beatrice she's in command of them.

"Look at what she's done!" Beatrice scrambles to her feet to face them. "Dad's service revolver! Gone!" Beatrice looks from face to face. Why are they staring at her that way? As if she's the crazy one? Charlie with too much to drink, and Kate, who knows if she's drunk or stoned, completely failed in her duty to keep Alfie off the hooch. And Evie who backs away, until she's behind them.

A flash of rage, James' words stumble back into Beatrice's head when she confronted him a few minutes earlier when he was in the lounge, recovering from Charlie's blow. Evie, he told her, one letter away from Evil. Nothing happened in the cabin, he told her. "I didn't succumb. Ask Alfie, he was there. He will tell you what kind of woman she is."

Why didn't you tell me, James? I would have understood. She wants to talk to James, on the far side of the deck. She faces Kate and Charlie. She steps across the deck, hoping to circle around them but Kate approaches her and Charlie follows Kate. Past them, Evie is frozen in place. But where is James?

"Beatrice?" Kate asks. "Are you okay?"

"Me? She hurt my hand!" Beatrice holds up the hand. Don't they see how red and bruised her hand is? The memory heightens the throbbing pain where her hand was kicked. Confusion in their faces. "You all saw her kick me. You're all witnesses."

"I think you need to lie down, Beatrice." Kate is within arm-reach.

"It's only my hand," Beatrice flexes the fingers. "I need that gun. But she's kicked it into the sea. Dad's favorite gun! She should be locked in the berth until we get her off."

"You're taking crazy, Beatrice," Charlie says, a few feet behind Kate. "Only one needs locking up is you."

"Me? Do you hear that, Kate? He's blaming me!" Beatrice incredulous, looks to Kate for support.

"Let's all stay calm," Kate asserts herself. "No one is getting locked up."

"Come on, Kate. Don't you see what's happening here?"

"Please, Beatrice," Kate replies.

"Maybe she and Charlie should be locked up," Beatrice continues. "How many of us will Charlie hurt because of her? First James, now Alfie. He'll take you and me down too if we oppose him. Isn't that right, Charlie? You want to beat me up?"

"I will if you don't calm down and shut up!" he snarls.

"You need to lie down, Beatrice," Kate says. "And Charlie, if you can't help the situation, shut the fuck up."

Kate and Charlie slowly advance on Beatrice. A couple dozen feet beyond them, Beatrice sees Alfie get to his feet. Alfie will take her side. James told her how Alfie will vouch for his story. Alfie agreed Charlie's girlfriend needed to be removed from the *Trinity*. Alfie had already changed their course to Port Angeles. Alfie hasn't been brainwashed by the sweet poison of Evie's seductiveness like Charlie and Kate have fallen in her web. Even without the revolver, Aflie will assert his authority and bring order.

Alfie on his feet advances toward Evie. Facing Beatrice, neither Charlie nor Kate sees him.

"We'll see what Alfie has to say about that," Beatrice says.

"Alfie is shit-faced," Charlie retorts.

"Alfie is still the captain, Charlie," Kate snaps, not turning from Beatrice.

"Maybe he's sobered up," Beatrice says. She raises her voice. "Alfie?"

Beatrice steps sideways to keep Aflie from falling out of view behind Charlie. She almost can't comprehend what happens, it comes so quickly. Evie rushes at Aflie as he stands near the rail. Alfie loses his balance. Alfie scrabbles desperately for something to hold on to. Beatrice sees it all too clearly. Evie's momentum as she shoves Alfie over the rail and off the side. Pushing Alfie off the yacht!

Beatrice blinks her eyes several times to confirm what she has seen. Alfie gone and Evie, at the far end of the deck near the rail, watches him drop.

Rage and fear flood into Beatrice; her mind turns red. Alfie murdered! Evie staggers back from where he fell, reeling from her horrible crime. Evie turns to look at the others, face a mask of panic, eyes wide and mouth agape, but that's all it is, a mask, an act, to make the others think it's an accident while Kate and Charlie miss the show, oblivious to what has happened as they continue to stare at Beatrice. Evie's feigned panic, the others be damned, Beatrice will have none of it, she will not be fooled.

"She's murdered him! Pushed him off the ship!"

"Beatrice?" Alarm in Kate's voice and widening eyes. "You're not well."

"She's getting all red again," Charlie adds. Neither he nor Kate comprehend what she has said.

"Me?" Beatrice steps away from them, thinking to sidestep them to get at Evie, who is still putting on her act of shock. "She killed Alfie! She will kill again if we don't lock her up! Why are you two so blind?"

"Calm down, Beatrice." Kate holds out her hands and comes towards her.

"Don't tell me what to do! Don't suppress me!" Beatrice looks to see how close she is to the rail. As she turns, she glances over at the narrow part of the deck by the helm bulwark and she sees that the gear cabinetry is open, and she can even see from her angle near the rail a part of the spear gun. She takes a few steps closer to get a better view. The spear gun in the cabinet, harpoon loaded.

What the hell? Did Evie leave it there, planning to use it on her later? Or Charlie perhaps, to threaten Alfie or James?

Her eyes freeze on it for a second or two, and then she turns to Kate and Charlie. They both follow her gaze, they see the speargun too. Beatrice makes a dash for it. Footsteps thunder against the wood of the deck.

"No, Beatrice!" Kate yells behind her.

"Stop her!"

They won't take this away from her. With the spear gun she can regain authority. Someone has to, now Alfie is gone. One needed force to retain civilization, to keep it from reverting to chaos and anarchy. Armed with the harpoon gun, she'd get Charlie and Kate to comply. They'd understand, even in their current madness. Maybe the speargun would snap them out of the spell the woman put into their heads. A jolt of fear.

Even Evie would understand, with the speargun pointed at her. Or would she? Would she comply with orders or would she dare Beatrice to pull the trigger? Beatrice only had one shot, no option for a warning. If Evie forces Beatrice to fire the speargun, Beatrice will have to make sure the shot counts. Not her fault if Evie forces her hand, is it? It's for the good of everyone aboard the *Trinity*, and Evie has already proved she's capable of murder, pushing Alfie off the side.

And poor Alfie, struggling to stay above the waves. Once Beatrice restores order with the speargun, she'll have them rescue Alfie. Turn the yacht around and . . .

These thoughts pass quickly through her head as she lurches towards the weapon. She bends to grab it out of the cabinet. The weapon practically leaps into her arms. Hands grasp to pull her away but her fingers tighten on the spear gun.

"Drop the fucking harpoon, Beatrice!" Charlie yells.

"Careful, Beatrice." A swirl of movement, the clatter of feet. She clutches the weapon, to keep them from grabbing it. The speargun jolts from her grasp with a sproing from the spring mechanism,

and a split second later the sound of a wet sloosh and loud thunk. She stares down at the speargun, the harpoon gone. Everything goes silent for a moment, except the unending wash of the sea.

In front of her Kate freezes, and Kate's eyes and mouth explode open and she screams. "Oh, my god!"

"Kate? Are you okay?" Beatrice lowers her gaze, past Kate's gaily colored swimsuit down to Kate's feet, clad in neon-orange flip flops to see that Kate appears uninjured. Still staring at Kate's toes, the orange pedicure complementing the orange footwear, she hears a raspy groan. She slowly moves her gaze to the left of Kate's feet, to Charlie's feet, next to the bulwark to the helm, the backs of his heels against the wall. Why is he standing with his back so close to the bulwark? She wills herself to look further up.

Blood on Charlie's naked chest. With difficulty Beatrice gazes higher, not quite sure what she is seeing, the grotesque image burns into her brain, an intensity to never be forgotten. Charlie's mouth is gaped open, eyes wide as he stands with his back flat against the bulwark. The tail end of the harpoon comes out of his mouth like an enormous tongue, the pointed end has ripped through the back of his head and pinned him to the bulwark.

"Charlie? Kate?" Beatrice doesn't know what else to say.

Charlie makes a noise, words failing to get past the spear to become grunts and moans, his teeth clacking against the metal spear.

"Look what you did!" Kate says. "I can't even . . ."

"Me? This isn't my fault." Beatrice shakes her head. How can Kate even think that? A fury twists darkly through Beatrice's head. Across the deck, Evie has her hands over her eyes. Beatrice points. "It's her fault! I told you we need to stop her! Help me reload the speargun." The speargun is on the deck a few feet away. She steps up to Charlie, to pull the harpoon out of the wall and his face, but he swats her away with his hands.

"Damn you, Charlie!" She spins to see Kate pick up the speargun. "We need to get another harpoon. Kate. What are you doing?"

Kate hurls the speargun off the side and looks at her defiantly. "No more of that, Beatrice."

"But we have to stop her! Look at what she's done." Past Kate, Evie appears in shock, standing near the center of the deck staring at Charlie. More acting, Beatrice thinks. Beneath the mask, she thinks Evie is laughing at them. First Alfie, now Charlie . . .

The *Trinity* lurches again.

"Beatrice, go up and steer!" Kate shouts. "No one is up there."

"No," Beatrice cries out. "You do it, Kate."

"I need to help Charlie."

Charlie has his hands around the shaft of the spear, trying to dislodge it from the wall.

"Damn you, Kate," Beatrice says.

As the vessel tilts more, an object slides across the deck, past Evie, fighting to keep her footing and towards Beatrice and Kate. Alfie's gun. Beatrice stares at it, and the others see it too. How did that get there after Evie kicked it over the side? The gun is only a yard from Evie's feet. Beatrice glances from the weapon to Evie's face, wondering again if Evie has the power of psychokinesis. And now Evie's brought the gun back up from the sea, and slid it almost to her feet. Evil powers, obtained through a pact with Satan. Evie looks down at the gun too.

"Oh, no you don't!" Beatrice dashes for the gun. Evie, frozen above it, as if maybe having been sapped of energy from dredging the gun out of the sea. So Evie has powers, but those powers aren't infinite. Evie reels back as Beatrice advances. Beatrice has her hands around the revolver but someone is on top of her.

"Beatrice, give it to me."

"No, Kate!"

The gun explodes. Kate cries out and falls. Beatrice stares at the gun in her hand and Kate in front of her. Evie scrambles to get away. "You'd better run," Beatrice says. Everyone is dying around her and Evie is escaping. Beatrice aims the gun at the fleeing woman and squeezes the trigger. The vessel lurches again. The bullet hits the bulwark, splinters flying. Evie reaches the hatch. Beatrice fires two more shots, unable to aim properly because of the unsteady yacht. Evie vanishes down the companionway to the cabin.

"Alfie! Alfie!" Kate screams hoarsely.

Beatrice turns to Kate. "Kate, are you okay?"

"I don't know." There is a hole in the bathing suit below her breast, a stain of dark spreading out on the fabric. Kate clutches her hand over the wound as she sits upright on the deck. "Beatrice, get me Alfie!"

"I don't know if I can."

"Beatrice, I'm scared. I don't think I've ever been this scared."

"You understand what's going on?"

"I don't know," Kate says. "Where is Alfie? Is he still lying in the lounge chair?"

"I don't think so, Kate."

"Is he up at the helm, steering?"

"No one is up there, Kate."

"No one is steering? Where is he?"

"I don't know, Kate."

"Find him. Wake him up if you have to." Kate yells again: "Alfie!"

Beatrice shakes her head. "I can't, Kate. He's dead."

"Dead? No. Tell me the truth."

"He went overboard, Kate."

"Overboard? Are you sure? You're not making this up?"

"She pushed him off the side, Kate. Didn't you see it?" Then she realizes Kate missed seeing Alfie fall in. But Kate must realize Alfie is gone, perhaps unwilling to accept the truth.

"Just bring him here, Beatrice. I don't care how drunk he is. And give me the gun before anyone else gets hurt." Kate reaches out her hand. Beatrice pulls the gun away from the grasping fingers.

"I need it. I need to get closer to her so I don't miss."

"Don't go yet, Beatrice." Kate's hand is on her leg.

Beatrice pushes the hand away. "I need to go."

"Beatrice, can I be honest with you. I never really liked you. You or James. I hate James. I only put up with you because of Alfie. But really, I never liked either of you." Kate speaks calmly.

"So you befriended this woman to destroy us? Is that it?"

"No. She's nothing to do with this."

"You can't protect her, Kate," Beatrice says. "I'll hunt her down and kill her." There's no other answer after Evie has stolen her meds and pushed Alfie off the side. Beatrice feels calmer now that she's made her decision, the storm in her mind rages at the periphery, but the center has a stillness, as she realizes what she has to do.

"Why, Beatrice?" Kate asks. "Why are you so full of hate?" Beatrice's attention is diverted. "Charlie?" she calls out. With the lurch of the *Trinity*, Charlie's head slides halfway down the shaft of the spear. It's hard to take her eyes off the grotesque tableau. Still pinned to the wall, he stands in a half crouch bent over, his hands out before him as if grabbing for something as he slowly lurches forward.

"There's evil in this world," Beatrice says. "That's what you can't see, Kate. You blind yourself to it. You and Charlie. And Alfie. Even James."

Kate doesn't seem to be listening to her, and Beatrice realizes Kate is dead.

Gun held in front of her, Beatrice stalks towards the hatch to the cabin, resolute with determination.

39: Alfie

Dazed, Alfie clutches to a rope. The icy water nips at his feet. He's flat against the hull of the *Trinity*, the deck a foot above him. All the haze from the booze and from the blow to his head when he fell off the helm, it all dissipates as a new urgency takes over. The adrenaline pours strength into his limbs as every memory of dangerous military service comes back to him. The panic that first gripped him is quelled, replaced by an exhilaration that pulses the need for action into every muscle in his body.

Just inches from his face, caught in the ropes, is his father's revolver. He lets go with one hand, reaches over and touches it, to verify it is not an illusion. Just curling his fingers around the handle pushes more strength into his arms. He will need the gun to keep order, once he gets above. He looks up at the gap of open deck between the railing. The gap is an inch above the reach of his hand, but with a small toss, the gun rattles onto the deck. Waiting for him.

Now to pull himself up over the railing. Grasping at a rope above his head, he tries to reach for the edge of the deck. His heart pounds in his ears. Heat and cold wrap misery into his arms and legs. Every effort shoots pain into his torso. His fingers still can't touch the lip of the deck. The strength he felt moments earlier begins to ebb into unendurable pain.

Maybe if he relaxes for a minute. Get his strength back up. Take some deep breaths and stay calm. He remembers he's no longer young, that image of Kate in the triangle bikini right before he fell over had made him think he was thirty-three again. If he was thirty-three, he'd have already pulled himself over the rail. Why isn't anyone helping him? He feels weak and tired. The pain intensifies in his fingers grasping the rope. Throbs of pain in his arms, legs, and head.

He begins to panic again. His heart slams like it's trying to break free from his chest, like that Alien movie. A pounding of pain that magnifies, erupting through every synapse and artery. An invisible dagger slashes into his chest, the abruptness jarring. The rigging pushes him away, flying upward as he falls. He grabs again but the ropes are out of reach. His feet hit something cold and hard, and the coldness is everywhere around him, as the *Trinity* blurs and wavers out of existence above like a dream about to be forgotten. The sun over his head slowly collapses into a yellowish smudge in the darkness that spreads over him. The sheer pain gives way to numbness, soothing and overwhelming as he descends into a darkening viscosity.

Darker and darker still. He realizes he is drowning. He is about to die. He's too tired to know if that's what he wants or if he should keep fighting. Just let it happen. Take me away from this hell.

40: Evie

Evie hears the bullet zing past her as she scurries down the steps to the cabin. It hits the side of the stairway in front of her, the hole popping into existence with a small shower of splinters. Two more bullets follow. She stumbles into the cabin, galvanized by fear.

Poor Charlie. The image will be in her head for the rest of her life, the shaft coming out of his mouth as if he was trying to swallow it, nailing him to the wall. His body writhing and squirming, like a bug stuck to a board. A stab of guilt that she couldn't help him, but was there any way to help? Beatrice tried to kill her. No question anymore, that is Beatrice's intent, and any minute Beatrice will burst into the cabin to hunt her.

Wide-eyed Evie sweeps the space searching for something to defend herself. Maybe the Walker empty or the other bottle which still has whiskey? Or something bigger, the urn with a picture of Charlie's dad. The confinement of the cabin feels like a trap, the walls closing in on her, the only other exit the steps at the far end, leading to the bow, out in the open where she'll be an easier target. The bedroom, the berth, as Charlie and Kate call it, if she could lock it from the inside, and hope the bullets can't penetrate the door.

She scurries quickly across the floor, reaching the door. She glances at the ladder to the front, but she imagines Beatrice coming around from the side deck, waiting to pick her off as soon as she sticks her head out.

Evie steps inside the berth. Behind the door, he leaps out. A hand grabs her shoulders, fingers dig in when she tries to pull away. James towers in front of her. The side of his face is bruised. He has a wide grin on his mug.

"Stop struggling!" James coos as his hand tightens and pulls her closer. "I want to help."

"Let go of me!" she hisses, pulling up her hand to slap him, but he grabs her wrist in his other hand.

"Calm down. I don't want to hurt you." He presses her up against the door. His battered face leers down at her.

"You are hurting me. Let go!" Her heart thunders in her chest.

"Does she still have the gun?" he asks.

Evie nods. "Please let go."

"Of course she does. That's why you ran down here. She's dangerous when she gets like this.

And with the gun . . . She'll kill us both unless we work together to stop her."

"How can I trust you?" she asks.

"You can't, except we're both dead if we don't work together."

"Then let me go."

"I don't trust you enough for that." James yanks her off the door and spins her around, his arm now around her neck, and his other hand twists her other arm up behind her back, shooting pain in her upper arm and shoulder.

"That hurts!" Evie cries out.

James eases the pressure. "I don't need to trust you until you show me I can trust you," he whispers in her ear. Her back against his firm body, he pushes her in front of him through the doorway into the main cabin, towards the dinette area.

"Are you sure she has the gun?" James asks.

"Yes," Evie answers.

"Why hasn't she come down yet? Maybe you killed her?"

"No. She's up there."

"You're not saying that?" He increases the pressure on her arm behind her back. "Lying to me?"

"No! Why would I lie about that?"

"That's it. Maybe you killed her after she killed Charlie." He walks her closer to the table. The damp towel on the table looks odd and from a few feet away, she sees it hides something underneath. James asks again: "Did you kill her?"

"No!" Evie exclaims. "She's up there with the gun."

"I don't think so. It's only you and me. You like that, don't you? I know I do. No one but the two of us. We can do what we want." James laughs as he continues to clutch her.

"I don't want this. Let go!."

His breath is hot on the back of her neck. "No point in pretending.

No one to tell us no." He presses her against the edge of the table and the hand behind her releases her wrist.

"I'm not lying. She's up there. She has a gun."

His free hand reaches past her to the table. Now or never she thinks, as she tightens her body. He pulls back the towel to reveal a knife with an eight-inch blade and ivory handle. As he reaches for the knife, Evie jolts sideways to propel an elbow jab to his gut.

"Ooof!" he gasps in pain. She grabs for the knife in front of her but he recovers too quickly, smacking her away before her fingers can touch the handle, while his other hand grasps at her bikini top and yanks hard. The fabric rips as she reels and spins off balance, stumbles across the floor, and falls on her hands and knees.

Evie looks up. James, the knife in his hand, nine feet away, facing her.

"You want to play rough? I can play rough too." He takes a slow step forward and another. She crawls backward until her feet hit the wall. He smiles at her from eight feet away. "Got you cornered. What a moment to savor." His eyes aim below her face. Without looking down, she's aware the bikini is in tatters at her upper arms and her breasts dangle exposed.

"Look at you. Makes me hard. See you like that." His free hand is in his bathing trunks, making an adjustment, and when he pulls his fingers out the erection is visible inside the trunks. "We can do this easy or we can do this hard. It's up to you, Evie. You have the power. I will get what I want, but you can choose how it goes."

"Do I have the power?" She gets to her feet and puts her hands over her breasts. "Get away from me."

"Or what?" he laughs. He takes a step closer.

Her back to the bulwark, she slides sideways a step. Her leg hits something heavy, the urn she realizes as she continues to face James. The knife pointed at her, his other hand on his crotch.

"She will be down here any moment, James," she says.

"Don't lie. She'd be down here already. You killed her, didn't you? Or did she kill herself? And Charlie's dead or you'd still be up there. Unless you prefer me to Charlie."

"Charlie is dead, but Beatrice is up there. She's armed."

James laughs. "Nice try. But enough foreplay. Why don't you remove the rest of the bikini? And take your hands away from your tits."

"No," she says.

"Fine. Like I said . . ." He goes into a crouch, now both hands in front as he moves towards her like a large predator stalking prey.

Fear surges through her. Evie bends down to grasp the urn, picks it up in both hands, and hurtles it at him. The twenty-pound urn hits the metal pole next to him and shatters into pieces. Shards fly everywhere as the cremated remains of Farley Mayhew break free from the confines of the urn, and erupt into a thick cloud of grayish white dust.

Glancing sideways, engulfed in the ash, James coughs and covers his eyes with one hand. A long thin shard of ceramic protrudes from his chest.

Evie backs away as the gray cloud wafts towards her. The ash fills most of the cabin; even in death Farley Mayhew has the need to dominate and control in the only way possible. Evie reaches the dinette, and from the half-open drawer, she grabs a knife, smaller than the one James has.

The voice is shrill. "What's all this smoke?" Flip-flop footsteps clatter. Through the haze, Evie sees Beatrice freeze at the bottom step. She has the gun in front of her, peering into the gloom that has enveloped much of the cabin.

"Beatrice?" James calls out.

"James, what's going on? All this smoke?"

"Not smoke," he says. "Ash." He pulls the shard out of his chest and drops it. He starts to slowly walk toward Beatrice.

"Ash? What do you mean?" Beatrice scans the room. She winces when she spots Evie, catching Evie's eyes for a second and pointing the gun at her. "Where's the..?" Beatrice turns pale. "What happened to Dad?"

"She threw the urn at me." James takes another step towards his wife. He has his hands at his side. The knife is tucked into the back of his swim trunks, Evie sees the hilt sticking out, and the imprint of the blade in the silk bathing trunks. James is in front and to the right of her, slowly moving towards Beatrice.

"What is going on here, James?" Beatrice asks.

"She was.. I pushed her away. Don't point that at me!"

"That's a lie!" Evie snaps. "He attacked me."

"Look at her," James says. "She threatened me if I didn't go down on her." He is seven feet from Beatrice, and Evie is another seven feet from him, moving closer to put him between Beatrice and herself while Beatrice steps sideways to widen the triangle the three of them form so that she can keep the gun trained on Evie as well as James.

Beatrice flicks the gun back and forth. "Stop moving or I shoot. Both of you."

"I'm telling you, Beatrice, it's her fault. Don't blame me." James takes another step. His hands at his side, one hand drifts backward, fingers inches from the knife hilt, out of Beatrice's view.

"I don't know if I can trust you, James," says Beatrice.

"Tell her to drop the knife," James replies.

"Tell him to drop his knife," Evie retorts.

"He doesn't have a knife, but you need to drop yours." Beatrice points the gun at Evie.

"He does!" Evie says.

"And poor Dad! The utter disrespect!" Beatrice glances past them to the ceramic shards on the floor, before focusing back on Evie. Beatrice's body shakes as she holds the gun in front of her in both hands, the barrel pointed at Evie's head. Beatrice speaks quietly and calmly. "You need to die."

Evie is paralyzed with fear. Staring at the barrel, a circle in front of her and below that Beatrice's finger tightening on the trigger, and beyond and above that, Beatrice's face, drained of emotion. No way can Beatrice miss.

Will I feel any pain? Or will it be over quickly, a blink of the eyes and I no longer exist?

41: James

James counted the gunshots. Two earlier when Alfie fired on the debris. Four more right before Evie ran into the cabin several minutes ago. He even checked to see the unopened box of ammo in the top drawer of the dresser in the berth. Alfie had not reloaded from when he fired the gun earlier. Beatrice has either forgotten the first two shots, or more likely hasn't paid attention and has no idea the gun is empty.

Four shots. How many of the others are dead? Or are they cowering in some corner of the yacht? Beatrice's face is red, her eyes rattling in the sockets, fully gripped with madness. All that madness focused on Evie, Beatrice points the gun at her and pulls the trigger.

James laughs at the look on Beatrice's face as the gun clicks impotently. He steps closer to her. She turns to him, her face full of hate. The fear floods back into him, even without the gun she is dangerous. Her fingernails, her teeth. As he approaches, he reaches for the knife behind his back. He might have to stab her to subdue her, he thinks. Self-defense is what it will be. She still has the gun in her hand. If anyone is alive above deck, they'll verify his story. She's armed with a gun, after all. How's he to know it's not loaded?

He realizes how much he loathes her. It happened over the last ten or fifteen years, building up, and he never wanted to admit it to himself. He would think it and hint at it with Charlie or his other friends, but he could never truly admit how he hated her.

Does he hate her enough to kill her? A widower makes out far better than a divorcee. And it seems easier. A divorce will be long and protracted; she will make sure it will be as agonizing as possible with all bridges burnt. It's not something he thinks he would have thought of, but now that the opportunity arises as if it is meant to be. It wouldn't be his fault. It will be self-defense. She has a gun, she's dangerous. What other choice does he have?

42: Evie

The gun clicks helplessly in Beatrice's hand. No flash from the barrel. Evie recovers from her shock. James pulls the knife from his trunks. Evie rushes at him with her knife, as he grasps his. Slams it hard into his back, the knife sinking to the hilt between some ribs. James gasps in pain and his knife clatters to the deck. The three of them stand there for a moment, James in between the two women and Beatrice eyeing Evie at the far side, and Evie holding on to the hilt of the knife, buried in James's back.

"You! What did you do?" Beatrice asks.

"He was going to stab you!" Evie replies.

It's like a dance, as Beatrice tries to get at her but James is in the way, the three of them for a moment twirl together, the cabin spinning around them, a carousel of craziness with James at the epicenter yelling in pain. Evie tries to pull the knife out, but the blade is firmly stuck, blood dribbling out of the wound.

"I will kill you!" Beatrice hisses. "You've destroyed our lives! Everyone dead because of you! Even my poor James!"

Evie lets go of the knife handle and backs away. James falls to the ground face-first. Beatrice reaches down to grab the knife, the handle sticking straight up from his back. She grunts as she pulls on it with both hands, but can't pull it loose. Evie is at the ladder to the bow. Footsteps rush towards her, as she scrambles up the steps. She glances back to see Beatrice has the knife James dropped and has almost reached her. Pulling herself out onto the deck, the knife knicks pain into her foot. On the bow, the sun's brightness throws her off guard for a moment after the dusky ash-filled cabin.

Beatrice hobbles up the ladder with the knife in hand. Evie rolls away from the hatch and gets to her feet. She runs and leaps and pulls herself on the roof of the cabin, the poop deck Charlie called it with a grin when they first came aboard. Beatrice emerges from below with the knife.

The yacht lurches, and the boom, groaning loudly, lunges at Evie. She falls on her side to avoid it, feeling it brush against her arm and thigh as it swings the sail to the other side of the vessel. When she tries to get up, her leg is trapped in some ropes that had shifted with the sail, a loop wrapped around her ankle. She is lying on the upper deck a couple feet from the edge, her body turned towards the bow.

On the bow in front of her, Beatrice regains her balance and picks up the knife. She looks around and pauses as she spots Evie on the upper level. She steps closer, her head level with Evie's, and sweeps her view to Evie's legs, and back to her face.

"Looks like you got tangled in the lines," Beatrice says. She brings the knife into view.

Evie nods, not sure how to respond. For a moment she thinks, maybe the madness has fled Beatrice. Maybe she realizes that Evie just saved her life, that James had the knife intending to kill Beatrice, and that in the next minute Beatrice will cut the ropes away from Evie's legs so the two of them can access damage and bring the yacht to safety. The madness of the last hour, or has it even been that? The concept of the passage of time abducted by trauma and violence, but perhaps the madness at what has happened will have broken through somehow, having been sated and Beatrice will see reason.

Evie has nothing else to do but hope. Lying on her side, her legs tangled in the ropes, one arm pinned beneath her, she can not defend herself.

"Please, Beatrice. We need to stop. Too much has happened already."

"It certainly has," Beatrice says. "This day was hell."

"I can't believe Charlie is . . ." Tears well up at the edges of Evie's eyes, blurring Beatrice and the bow behind her. With her free hand, she wipes the tears.

"Dead. Charlie was my little brother. And even if we didn't always see eye to eye, I loved Charlie. Do you realize that? I loved Charlie!"

"I did too, Beatrice. Very much. And he loved you too. He didn't know how to show it, but he loved you."

"You?" Beatrice narrows her eyes. "What do you know about love, you little skank? Because of you, everyone I know is dead. You made my life hell. Now I'll make your life hell." She points the knife at Evie's chest. Evie sticks her hand in front of her, not that it would be any defense against the knife blade. Beatrice jabs the knife. The blade nicks the side of Evie's hand, and she draws it back, a slash at the palm near the pinkie finger.

"So, you bleed red," Beatrice says. "I almost wondered if you were a demon or something."

The yacht lurches again, and the boom flies back around, above Evie lying down and Beatrice's head. Beatrice grabs the edge of the cabin roof to keep herself steady.

"Hasn't there been enough misery?" Evie says. "No one is steering the yacht."

"Enough misery? You inflict it on us and then you want to decide it's enough?" Beatrice lets out a cold, bitter laugh.

"I didn't inflict it. I didn't do anything."

"All lies. None of this would have happened."

Beatrice shifts her position, closer to Evie's legs, and pokes the knife again. Evie flinches as the blade licks her thigh. Another sharp throbbing pain.

"What the fuck is wrong with you?" Evie asks.

"What the fuck is wrong with you? Showing my husband your tits like a brazen whore. You are one sick puppy."

"He attacked me. I wanted nothing to do with him."

"When you flaunt your body topless, what do you expect? You lure him away, jiggling those around until he doesn't want to see my empty wine sacks. How many times did you and James fuck?"

"Never!" Evie insists. "I only met him Tuesday."

"I don't believe you. Everything you say is a lie." Beatrice jabs again with the knife. Evie sees the slash of red, on her thigh before she feels the pain blossom inside her leg. It doesn't even hurt as much as the other one.

"I suppose you can't help the way you are," Beatrice says. "A shit father. A loser mother. Trash. No family to speak of. In earlier centuries you'd have been covered in shit, but because of modern plumbing, you have a modicum of a chance to pass as one of us. No matter what we give you, your kind will always want more. Share and share alike, because you are all too lazy and stupid and low-born to work hard and make it rich. Charlie says you are a socialist like him. He just did it to piss off Dad. To get at Dad's goat, but Dad was stoic, he put up with all Charlie's bullshit. Dad would have . . ." Beatrice stiffens. "Dad? Poor Dad! You desecrated his remains."

"I'm sorry. James was trying to . . ."

"Shut up!" Beatrice bursts. Another lunge with the knife, but Evie flinches enough that the blade is a cold nip on the skin and doesn't puncture it, a welt on her breast.

"Haven't enough people died, Beatrice?"

"The men are putty in your hands, aren't they? They take one look at you and . . ." Beatrice shuts her eyes. "I remember when I was young and James looked at me that way. He was only twenty-three and I had just gotten my divorce. They made fun of me for robbing the cradle, even though Alfie was older than me and Kate younger than James. He hadn't had much experience, and I was beautiful at thirty. He was more in love with me than I was with him back then. But I realized I was already thirty, and I didn't want to remain single and pathetic when my first husband married a girl three years younger than me, so I married James to spite him. But then after fifteen years, I realized how much I loved James and needed him. Fifteen years.

"Meanwhile, I think during that time he fell out of love with me. The more time I spent with someone, the more I couldn't bear to be with anyone else, whereas I could sense he was getting bored with familiarity. He wanted something new. I could sense it inside me, even if I never talked to him about it, or could even accept it myself. But it was there" Beatrice has tears in her eyes.

Evie doesn't know what else to do. She looks at Beatrice imploringly, mentally saying: have mercy on me have mercy on me. To say anything aloud threatens another knife slash. A crazy thought takes hold of her. To do anything is better than nothing, no matter how silly. A mantra to quell the pain and fear, and maybe to break through to Beatrice. Mental vibrations in her head. Drop the knife, Beatrice. Squeeze the madness away. You will only be sorry tomorrow. Help me out of these ropes. We will take the yacht to the nearest port for help. It is all a bad accident. We'll tell them pirates boarded the ship, and they slaughtered everyone else while we hid under the bed in the berth, you and I, Beatrice, holding each other's hands. One of them stabbed at the bed, that's how I got these wounds. Maybe they were mad at your dad, a man like him must have had enemies.

If only Evie can get through to Beatrice, let her know there are many roads, and Beatrice should weigh consequences but Beatrice is still hellbent on one path where Evie is tortured and killed.

"Stop looking at me like that!" Beatrice says. "You're so pathetic. Is that the look you give to the social welfare clerk? I want to cut that face off of you." Another knife slash at Evie's face. Evie puts up her hand and twists away.

"Fuck!" Another gash, at the center of her palm. This woman would cut her slowly into pieces. This could go on for hours. Kill me now so I don't have to hear you drone on. This black humor in her mind makes Evie grimace. She pushes herself up on her elbow, her head is above Beatrice's.

She looks at the slash in her palm and it makes her think of Jesus, a nail in the hand, must have felt something like this, and she knows Jesus is an imaginary friend that wasn't coming here now to save her, a fraud, not that she ever believed in religion.

"Beatrice, stop it!" Evie says. "Look at me!"

"No! I won't have you poison my head like the others."

"Please, Beatrice. Listen to reason. Charlie is hurt! And Kate! We have to help them. And go back to look for Alfie before he drowns."

"You killed them!" Beatrice says.

"No!" Evie cries out.

"You lie! You killed James!"

"No. He tried to kill you. He had the knife. He was about to stab you."

"James? He cheated on me. You and him."

"No. He attacked me."

"Poor James."

"Poor James! He fucking tried to kill you, Beatrice."

"No, he would never . . ."

"You know it's true," Evie says. "You said yourself, he was tired of you. You don't have to like me, but you have to believe me, Beatrice. There's no one else left."

"No one left. I don't want to be alone." Beatrice's eyes begin to become clear, her face softening.

"I don't either. We need to go get help. To see if we can save Charlie and Kate. And James."

"Yes. To see if we can get help."

"Get the *Trinity* to the nearest port. You know how to sail the *Trinity*, don't you?"

"Yes," says Beatrice. "I can sail it. I feel like this has been a bad dream."

As they talk, Evie spots movement on the floor. A torso and a pair of legs slide across the deck behind Beatrice, leaving a smear of red. Charlie? Evie thinks. She can't imagine what Charlie's face would look like once they pull out the harpoon, his charming looks will become hideous, and even though she'll love him, he'll think she wants someone who doesn't look like a freak.

Not Charlie, she realizes, James. He speaks up. "Beatrice, put down the knife."

43: Evie

As Beatrice begins to turn a gunshot shreds the quiet. Her face is jerked back towards Evie as the cheek and an eye explode. Blood splatters in a spray of droplets, hitting Evie like rain on a windy day. Shocked look on what is left of Beatrice's face, she crumples and falls out of view to reveal James on the deck seven feet behind her, on one hand and knees, the other hand holding Farley's gun. The knife is still in his back, and a trail of blood runs along the deck heading back to the side deck where he came from. The knife, released from Beatrice's hand, lies on the edge of the cabin roof, blade towards Evie, balanced precariously but within reach of Evie.

"You . . . you murdered her!" Evie gasps.

"I . . . I didn't mean to pull the trigger." James's face is pale with fright. "As much as I hated her . . . you don't realize the hell she put me through, these last several years. I wanted her to drop the knife, and then I got afraid when she started to turn."

The knife in front of her, Evie is afraid to reach past the blade for the handle. Will James shoot her too if she tries? He has the gun lowered, on the deck. If she was an action hero in a story, she'd grab the knife and hurl it at him before he drew a bead and fired, the image of the knife in his throat and the gun slipping away from his fingers, but she is not that person.

"Push the knife down here," James says as if he can read her thoughts.

"I need to cut the ropes. My leg is tangled."

"I don't like the idea of you and knives. Not with the one in my back."

"You were about to stab her. That's why I did it."

He shakes his head. "I was going to disarm her. That's all."

"You knew the gun was empty," Evies says.

James nods. "It's not empty now." Groaning, he gets up on his knees to get a better angle to view her over the lip of the cabin roof. With his hands together holding the gun, he'd look like he's in prayer if his eyes weren't open. "I told you to push the knife off. I don't trust you."

"Don't point that at me," Evie says. "What if you shoot again by accident? If that's what it was."

"It was an accident. I swear it was."

"I don't believe you, James."

"You have to, Evie. It's just you and me. You have to trust me. I'm the only way you get out of this alive."

"Then trust me. My foot is caught. I need to cut away the ropes."

"I don't know." James's brow stitches together as he contemplates. The yacht shifts, and the boom groans and lunges towards her. She falls back against the deck as it rushes over her to the other side. The knife slides and teeters before it falls out of view and thumps quietly on something softer than the deck.

James forces a smile on his face. "Now that that's settled. Why don't you climb down?"

"I told you. I can't. My leg." She lifts up part of her leg, snaggled in the lines, though less so, she realizes when the boom shifted sides.

"You owe me something, Evie," James says. "I saved your life and you stabbed me in the back."

"You murdered her, James. You need to confess. Atone to God for mercy."

"Come on. I know you don't believe in that bullshit, and neither do I." James chuckles. "I told you it was an accident. I feel bad for her. I really do." His voice chokes up, and his eyes are watery with tears. "But I needed to be free of her. I didn't want it to happen this way. She was so insecure. Every time I'd hint at divorce, she'd get in this hyper state. Her dad and her first husband were both abusive to her. At least I wasn't that. I was a good husband. But I couldn't keep living this way. I was too young when I married her. She's taken almost half my life. I couldn't lose any more of it. The missed opportunities. I was desperate for change. When you flirted with me, Evie . . ."

"I didn't flirt with you."

"You did. The other day. And even today. I see it in your face. This family is crazy, Evie. Every one of them, Charlie too. Subconsciously I think you know that, and you want a way out. You want me, Evie. No, stop shaking your head like that. You want me as much as I want you."

"No!" Evie hisses.

"It doesn't matter now," James continues. "You can stop pretending. Charlie's gone. They are all gone. Come down here and be with me. Now that I've saved your life. You owe me that."

"I can't! I'm trapped up here."

"You owe me. You stabbed me in the back. I'll probably die soon, I've lost a lot of blood. You owe me something. Take your arm away from your tits. Maybe you can . . . pull down your bikini panties and . . ."

"No! I can't!"

"Yes, you can! Pull them down from your thighs. I want to watch you masturbate yourself. I want to die with a nice image in my head. You won't do that for me?"

"No!" She feels sick with revulsion.

"I suppose you're just like her. Charming at first, and then you turn hateful. Fucking bitch! I saved your damn life. You fucking stabbed me in the back. Literally. You owe me!"

"I owe you nothing," Evie says.

"I don't want to hurt you, but if I have to, I will. Don't make me come over there. I'm getting what I want, one way or another."

Evie shakes her head. What else can she do? James sighs and starts to get on his feet. He cringes as he goes erect, staggering backward to the edge of the bow as he struggles to keep the gun aimed at her. His face is white and his eyes begin to lose focus, and he brings the gun in closer to his chest. He falls face forward.

His body thumps loudly, and the gun goes off beneath him, jerking his head upward as his jaw is ripped out of his skull to fly into the wall beneath her and clatter back into view on the deck a few feet away from him. His eyes stare up at her for a moment from the bloody remains of his head, now jaw-and-chinless, before the head smacks down onto the deck. A puddle of red begins to spread on the deck around his head, a halo of blood.

Evie lies down, taking deep breaths, trying to remove the horror from her head, the grisly images of Charlie, Beatrice, and James seared and branded deep into her brain. What now? Everyone is dead. Alfie drowned like Captain Ahab, Charlie harpooned and the others shot. The decks of the *Trinity* awash in red. She the only survivor. She pulls at her leg, to get it freer from the ropes. But what can she do? She doesn't dare go to the bow, with the grotesque corpses of James and Beatrice, and even if she crawled over to the back, more corpses to confront her on the main deck. Even if she makes it to the safety of the helm, she doesn't know how to operate the yacht, which any of the others could manage, she thinks with a bitter irony.

As she lies back on the cabin roof, some dark clouds break the serene blue of the sky. I can't lie here forever. The yacht lurches again and the boom swooshes over her as she flattens against the deck. Much easier to let it sweep her aside like debris, knock her into the water, but she can't give up. The urge to live, the urge to survive, her mind racing with fear and sadness but a desire to keep going.

At least I'm alive. Until the yacht sinks or I die of starvation or . . . The *Trinity* lurches again, the boom sweeping over her, and now the deck leaning more to one side. What to do when you know you're going to die? There's nothing to prepare one.

Is she going to die? On her back, the ropes at her legs. More gray clouds above. She sees shapes in the clouds. One shape and another, a deer's face becomes a shark as the cloud changes. The memory of lying in the grass and looking up at the clouds and finding different creatures, dinosaurs, and fantasmas. A string of good memories.

"Evie, are you okay?" Charlie leans over her. His face completely healed. No, she's drifted to sleep, a dream. She looks over to see Alfie climb up onto the front of the bow. She doesn't know how much time has passed, but she can't lie and wait. She needs to get to the helm. She pulls herself up and stumbles to the lower deck before the boom can swing again.

The side deck is smeared with blood from one end ot the other. She steps past Beatrice to enter the cabin. The ashes have mostly settled, the interior coated in a thin layer to make the whole space eerie and colorless; Charlie's father's last attempt to dominate. She shakes the white dust off her pack and grabs her cellphone from the side-pocket. No signal. The ship veers and swings to the other side, and she loses her balance. An image on the floor in front of her stares at her from a triangular shard of ceramic, Farley Mayhew, his image clear of the ash, his expression uncompromising. He won't admit he bore such awful progeny, he won't tell her he's glad Charlie had found love.

She will have to make her way past the swash of blood James left on the steps to the main deck. She can't bear to look at Charlie, but cannot avoid seeing him, half slid off the spear bent forward with his hands below him, as if reaching for something in front of him, chasing an allusive goal.

He makes a noise. The vessel lurches and the spear and the wall make a loud crack. The spear breaks loose and Charlie is propelled face forward. The spear beneath him erupts out of the back of his head as he lands, a gusher of blood at the base while the spear above his head is like a mast.

And Kate. Laid out on the deck, a single clean bullet hole in her bathing suit, a slow stream of blood at her side, neat and clean in death the way she led much of her life.

Evie climbs to the helm. She has no idea what to do, but she slumps into the captain's chair, the wind in her face, the sails luffing loudly above her. Captain of a floating tomb. Nothing to do but wait and hope and imagine she's somewhere else. The stories she will tell when and if she gets out alive. She can only believe she will survive because anything else would be intolerable. She will survive and she will thrive. The poison that doesn't kill you makes you stronger.

To her right, she thinks she sees a sash of far-away lights, maybe Port Angeles. But how to get the vessel to move that way? She looks down at the controls. Alfie showed her the throttle and the start button. She pushes the button and lifts up on the throttle, and to her amazement, the engine rumbles to life somewhere below. With one hand on the wheel, she tries her phone again, to see if it has service while slowly pulling on the wheel, directing the boat towards the far-away lights.

Grave Incident

1: Fifteen hours after

Sam enters the bedroom with a cup of coffee. Chloe is in the armchair by the window, looking at the apartments across the street. He places a cup on the windowsill near her. She remains frozen, not looking at him or the coffee. Sam clears his throat.

"They caught him," he says.

"Huh?" She looks up, confused. Her eyes are tear-blurred and blood-shot.

"Spike. I saw it on my computer while the coffee was brewing. His real name is Barus Jones."

"Barus Jones," she repeats the name slowly. "I knew that." She looks down at the cup of coffee and slowly reaches for it.

"It's on the Portland news sites."

She doesn't reply. She takes a sip and places the mug back on the sill.

"They caught him," he says. "It's over."

"I don't think so. It's just begun. I don't think it will ever be over."

"We need to move on, Chloe."

"I can't move on. I can't erase it from my head, Sam."

"Maybe we can do something this afternoon," he says. "A distraction? Go to the museum?"

"No! Why don't you take Lacey and leave me alone." She sips more coffee and continues to stare out the window. Sam follows her gaze to the red brick facade of the adjoining building. Most of the windows have the blinds down. He sighs, walks back to the kitchen, and refills his coffee cup. Not that he needs more caffeine, his nerves already jittery.

With his cup of coffee, he goes up to the roof deck. Sprawled on a chaise lounge, Lacey stares out at the rooftops. A fifth of whiskey is on the table next to her coffee.

"Want some sweetener in your coffee, Sam?"

Sam glances over at the door to the stairs. "Sure," he mutters. She uncaps the bottle and reaches over to pour a generous portion in his cup.

"They caught him," he says.

She nods and stares at him. "I saw that. I guess that's good."

"Isn't it?"

"I don't know. Don't want to think about it. I want to go home, but now I'm stuck."

"You never liked him. No reason to stay."

"I should stay for Mother. But I can't stand it here, with Chloe like that."

"She's upset," he says.

"We're all upset. How come you're so calm?" She stares at him.

"I'm upset too."

"I hope she pulls out of it. Another fucking week. I can't stand it here."

"How about Lenox?" he suggests.

"Are you kidding? That dump? Especially after . . ." She shudders.

"What happened yesterday?" he asks.

"Why don't you ask her? She's your intimate partner, not me." She tosses this at him with a flirt of her head that pushes the robe ajar.

He gazes, suddenly thinking life is too overwhelming as he thinks how attractive she is, more sure of her attractiveness than Chloe, which makes her seductive. Not that he would act on it, not with Chloe one floor below. "Why is she acting this way?" he asks. "What really happened up there?"

"Sam, you already know. But bring it up again and traumatize her even more."

"I don't know what to say to her. They caught Spike and she's still . . ."

"Deal with it, Sam. That's all we're trying to do right now. Never seen her this bad. Me, I'll drink the next few days to get through it." She takes a drink of coffee and lies back in the chair with her robe open exposing black lace panties and bra.

"So that's the answer?" he asks.

"Why not? Distraction. Drinking. Can't think of anything else. Can you?"

She does that flirty toss of her hair again. He can't look at her without his eyes trailing down her torso to her legs, and this makes him uncomfortable. You must relish making me feel this way, he thinks.

He sighs. "I better go down and check on her."

"Maybe you better," Lacey replies.

2: Thirty-two hours before

It has been two years, and Chloe is excited and nervous to see her sister emerge from the security gates at Portland International Airport.

"Chloe!" Lacey rushes towards her, followed by a large leather Louis Vuitton suitcase on a leash.

They give each other a long hug.

"So glad you're here, Lacey," Chloe gushes. "Wasn't sure you would."

"And miss the funeral?" Lacey laughs. "It'll be nice to see Mom, though. And I miss you, Chloe. If not for you I wouldn't be back. Couldn't go through this without you. You're the one sane person in the family."

"You make it easier for me too," Chloe says.

"Half a day, get the family bullshit over and the rest of the trip will be fun."

"Sam has the car." Chloe pulls out her phone. "He's looping around. I'll let him know you arrived." They reach the escalator. On the ride down she texts Sam. "You won't recognize Portland, Lacy. It's changed. A lot of new places."

"Can't wait. I've heard about all these great restaurants."

"Wish you could stay longer."

Lacey shrugs. "We'll see. Might push it another two or three days, if the tickets don't cost too much to change."

3: Fourteen hours after

"You want coffee?" Sam asks quietly. Chloe lies in the bed, curled in a fetal position beneath the blankets. "Chloe?"

"Let me be," she moans.

He shrugs and plods back to the kitchen where the electric drip machine has just filled the glass pot. He pours himself a coffee and sits at the kitchen nook, with his laptop open.

Several minutes later, he hears a woman's voice from the hallway. Bare feet slap the floor, getting louder. Chloe's sister Lacey stumbles in, bloodshot eyes and tangled hair, wrapped in a bathrobe.

"Did you make coffee?" she asks.

"Help yourself." He points to the coffee machine on the counter. She takes a cup off the wooden rack, pours herself some, and sits down at the table close enough he can reach out and touch her. She pulls her phone from a pocket in the robe and starts tapping on it.

"You talk to your mother?" he asks.

She nods. "Figure I better, since Chloe won't. She still sick?"

"If that's what you call it. I feel like she and you are keeping something from me."

Lacey shrugs. "You need to ask her."

"She won't tell me anything."

"Some of this is your fault, too. You should have warned us when he got there. None of this would have happened the way it did."

"I didn't know what was going on," Sam says. "I came as soon as I could,"

"You should have been there."

He takes another sip of coffee. "What happened, anyway?"

"Why don't you ask Chloe?"

"She's in no condition to tell me anything."

"I can't say any more," Lacey says. "If I start to tell what Chloe has kept from you, those secrets will bind me and you. It'll create an intimacy between us that might tempt me further. I can't do that to Chloe. Maybe when I was younger, but . . ." She looks up at him. "Unless you're ready to burn bridges now that you've seen the family madness."

Sam shakes his head. "No. I love Chloe."

"I almost believe you, Sam." Cup of coffee in hand, she stands. "I'm heading up to the roof."

4: Twenty-five hours before

Sam looks up from his magazine at the sound of the door. Chloe and Lacey walk in, each carrying a cloth re-usable grocery bag. The tops of a couple bottles of wine poke out of one bag.

"We're back," Chloe announces. "You done with work?"

"Finished half an hour ago," he replies. "We can leave any time."

"We were thinking of dining out here. That new brewery on Broadway?"

"Before we go to Lenox?"

"Otherwise Mother will want to take Lacey to that dreadful steakhouse," Chloe says.

"The one with the animals on the wall?" Sam asks.

Chloe nods and walks past him into the kitchen area, and Lacey follows.

"Animals on the walls?" Lacey queries.

"Yeah," Chloe replies as she places items from the bags on the counter. "Their heads. Old, moth-eaten heads. Gazelles and deer. Staring down sadly while you eat. It's what makes for fine dining in Lenox, Washington."

"I don't suppose they have a vegetarian alternative?"

"Hell no, Lacey! They put meat in the salads. I wouldn't be surprised if the desserts all had bacon."

After the women put away groceries, Chloe comes back out. "Sam? We're going to pack our stuff in the car now and leave from the restaurant. So we get to Lenox before dark."

He nods. "I'm already packed."

"We'll probably stay tonight and tomorrow. Drive back Sunday after breakfast."

"I don't need to work until Monday afternoon. And if Lacey hasn't seen the family . . ."

Chloe shakes her head. "One full day in Lenox is enough. For me and for Lacey."

He nods. He knows how emotional she gets when she goes home to her family. He'd gone several times with her, Christmas and Thanksgiving, and a couple of other times during the year and a half together, always an over-night, or for the day, to visit her mother, her older sister, and brother, but never the father, though the father lived there, a remote house up a dirt road, until he was hospitalized several weeks ago. Now the father is dead and visiting him is no longer an issue, except this one last time for the service.

"We leave in one hour." She turns to her younger sister. "Lacey?"

"Huh?" In the kitchen, Lacey looks up from her phone.

"We leave in an hour?"

"Sure, Chloe."

5: Two hours thirty minutes after

Sam is convinced he's on the wrong road driving deeper into nowhere. Nothing is familiar in the darkness. The silence in the car and the sameness of the passing curves in front of them, the dreary gray of the headlights hitting past woods, eats into his head.

"It's so damn dark!" Sam explodes. Chloe mutters under her breath. From the back seat Lacey stares at him in the rear view mirror, but he can't read the emotion on her face. He clutches the steering wheel and continues onward through the darkness. Chloe knows the road better than him, but she is hunched up in the seat, a hoodie pulled over her head.

A moment later he sees a blur of light on the horizon. Trees fall away and they emerge into an opening. The interstate glows in the distance.

"I-5 up ahead. What a relief," he sighs.

Is it a relief? The car is still thick with tension. Neither Chloe nor her sister speak. Chloe is still catatonic and Lacey catches his eye every time he glances at the rear-view.

The lights play across her sullen face, as they near the on-ramp. He doesn't dare turn on the radio, even here, in range of some good Portland stations. With a deep breath, he steps on the gas to merge on the interstate bereft of traffic at this hour, a few dots of red ahead and pairs of white glow behind. Even this late, the vehicular artery of the region pumps with life.

"Whew!" he sighs. "That relieves some tension."

Lacey mutters something over the engine drone, the only word he makes out is "tension."

Chloe bolts upright. "Lacey, shut up!"

"Chill, Chloe!"

"What did Lacey say?" Sam asks.

"Like you pretend you didn't hear, Sam. Always pleading ignorance."

"No. What did she say?"

"You want to know? She said she knew what would relieve her tension and she was looking right at you when she said it."

"That wasn't what I meant at all, Chloe," Lacey snaps. "Don't let mom put stupidity in your head. She means well, but shit . . ."

"And, Sam, you looked back at her through the rear-view," Chloe continues. "I saw the way you shot your eyes up and back from the mirror, and you sucked in your breath when she said it."

Sam looks over at her for a moment. He is completely empty of words or emotion. No one says anything. Sam hears a rustle of clothing, like large moths trapped in a cloth bag. When he looks at Chloe again, she is hunched forward buried beneath the hoodie.

"We need to stay calm. Ride this out." Sam's voice is a whisper. "I don't think we have anything to worry about."

"Will you shut up!" Lacey hisses from the back seat.

Chloe sighs loudly.

Sam looks ahead at the ribbon of highway. It seems anything he brings up will erupt in an outburst, jarring more stress and angst into him. Back and forth, his body buffeted in the volley of words. Followed by interminable silences, before he dares to speak again, simply to calm his nerves.

He keeps his voice low. "Everything will be alright."

"You don't know," Lacey says. "What if he follows us to Portland?"

He doesn't reply. Maybe the police will catch Spike first, he wants to say, but he tightens his lips and concentrates on the highway, more traffic as they near Vancouver.

6: Twenty hours before

"Finally," Chloe remarks.

"Entering Le Knocks" Lacey adds.

From the back seat, Sam sees the sign at the side of the road: "Entering Lenox, Washington, Population 5,168." They'll need to reduce that number by one he thinks to himself.

He leans towards the front seat. "We timed it perfectly. Not yet nightfall."

"Takes forever to get here," Lacey says. "Though it's, what, seventy miles from Portland."

"Less than that, I think," Chloe replies.

"When's last time you been home, Lacey?" Sam asks.

"Chicago is home," Lacey humphs. "Not this shit-hole."

"You know what I mean."

"Five years. Maybe I'll visit more often. Now that he's not around."

"That'd be lovely, Lacey," Chloe says.

Lacey stares at the passing buildings. "Why I put off coming back. The obligation to come here. I didn't miss anything. Place hasn't changed. Still a dump."

They have been in a gay mood since Lacey arrived that morning, and even mention of their father's funeral has not deflected Chloe's contentedness. Chloe got tense and moody those other trips to Lenox, but now she and Lacey bubble with giggles and conversation, as they drive through downtown, past a grocery, diner, general store, tavern, thrift store, a couple more shops and businesses, a restaurant, and a gas station, straddled along three blocks. All but the gas station and tavern are closed, and even those look dead.

"Lenox remains stuck while time moves on," Chloe says. "Still, mom will be glad you're here."

"I think I'm ready for Mom. Look past the stupid things she says. I won't let her head-fuck me."

"Lacey!" The vehicle shrieks to a halt. They are at the intersection in front of the general store, where the town's one traffic light blinks yellow. A large man crosses the street in front of them. The man stares into the car window as he struts slowly as if he owned the street. He rubs his finger across his exposed tongue.

"Fucking Spike. What a fucking asshole!" Lacey remarks. "Chloe?"

"I'm okay," Chloe says quietly. "Not letting anyone ruin my evening. Not even him."

"Who is he?" Sam asks.

"A loser," Lacey answers. "Does he still live in that trailer on Oak Street?"

"Let's not talk about it." Chloe continues to drive. They turn up the next street, and three blocks further, with woods on one side, they are on the dead-end street a hundred yards from Mother's. Lacey fires up a joint.

"Some rituals never die," Sam muses.

"She condemns pot, even though most of the time she's bonkers on pills and alcohol. You want some, hon," Chloe twists sideways in the driver seat to reach the joint back to him.

"Sure."

When the joint shrinks to where one can't take a hit without burning thumb and index finger, Lacey pops it into a metal Altoids tin. Chloe starts the car, pulls into the driveway, and switches it off again.

"Well, here it goes," Lacey says. She opens the door and climbs out.

"Sam, will you bring in our things?" Chloe gets out and follows Lacey across the parched yard to the front door of the manufactured home.

Sam drags Chloe's vinyl duffelbag and Lacey's soft leather Louis Vuitton out of the trunk of the car. There's also bottles of wine and a bag of snacks, a chip and veggie assortment, but he will make a second trip.

7: Two hours after

From her recliner, Gladys Emerald watches her two daughters and Sam depart. What is wrong with Chloe? Too sick to be traveling. She hopes Chloe isn't upset that she mentioned the time Lacey stole Chloe's boyfriend. She didn't mean to blurt it out. So stupid of her! But it was a long time ago, and now the two sisters have different lives in different cities. Why are kids so sensitive these days?

The car drives away, and she turns off the band-era hits, hoping to hear the car return. She waits in silence. When she grabs her walker to get up, the clock on the cocktail table falls to the floor. The cord must have tangled with the walker somehow, and she strains to pick up the clock, now blinking twelve am. She goes to the bedroom to look at the other clock.

Past nine. She's surprised. How quickly time passes. Two and a half hours, just like that, and she thinks she should be more distressed at Chloe's predicament, but she has enough troubles of her own, and she is old and tired. She wants to relax and she wants everyone around her to be agreeable and polite.

She considers calling Mark, as she knows he has taken his father's death hard. She expected him to check on her and ask how the day had gone. It has gone well until this unexpected situation with Chloe.

She wants company, and she thought the girls would be around to talk with her and that Mark would join them for a couple hours, where they'd comfort each other on this sad day. Instead she is alone, her children deserting her.

8: Nineteen hours forty minutes before

"Lacey!" their mother yells over the loud country and western blaring from the TV. She mutes the sound. She is ecstatic as she watches them enter. "Lacey!" she says again from her recliner. "Come here, darling! Been so long! Come give your mother a hug!"

"Finally made it, Mother," Lacey walks to their mother.

"You look good, Lacey. My big city daughter."

"You look good too, Mom."

"You kids hungry? Too late for the steakhouse, but there's sandwiches in the fridge. I bet Sam is hungry."

"No. We ate before we left," Chloe says. "But we brought wine. I'll have Sam pour some after he brings in the luggage."

"I hope you stay the week, Lacey. Or longer, to make up for lost time."

"Just the weekend, Mom. Depends on Sam's schedule," Lacey replies.

"I want to take you girls and Sam to the new steak house. It's real fancy. You remember that place, Chloe, where I took you and Sam?"

"I'm sure it's real nice, mother," Lacey says as she tries not to laugh at Chloe's eye-roll.

"Big servings, not like that place Chloe took me to in Portland, a tiny bit of food lost on a huge plate, and the prices!"

"I guess it beats the Burger Barn," Lacey chuckles.

"You kids used to love Burger Barn."

Both Chloe and Lacey hold their necks with gagging and choking motions.

The sisters sit on the sofa along one wall, and the three women discuss the past, names of relatives and people from the school and the town, unfamiliar names to Sam who half-listens to them. He enters the adjoining kitchenette and opens the drawers until he locates the cork-screw wine-opener. After he pours four glasses of wine, he brings them out and hands one to each woman.

"Why, thank you, Sam." Their mother gleams. "Chloe caught a nice one, don't you think, Lacey?"

"Mom!" Chloe groans.

"Yeah, he's okay," Lacey says.

"He's a real keeper. And they're getting married next summer. You'll be back out, Lacey?"

Lacey glances at Chloe questioningly. "Of course I will. Wouldn't miss it."

"We haven't yet decided on that, Mom," Chloe interjects.

"Well, you'd better, before someone else steals him." The mother looks at Lacey as she says this. "And we need something to look forward to, bring the family together. A wedding. Better than a funeral."

"Are you going, mom?"

"Of course I will."

"No, I mean the funeral?"

"Yes, Lacey. Why would you ask?"

"Just that you and him haven't been married in . . ."

"That doesn't matter. Because we divorced doesn't mean I won't go. So, how about you, Lacey?"

"Huh, mom?"

"Are you seeing anyone?"

"I see a lot of people every day," Lacey says.

"Lacey, that's not what I meant."

"I'm too busy, mom."

"Too busy? You and Chloe aren't getting any younger. No one wants an old nag."

"Mom, please!" Chloe groans.

"I want my daughters to be happy. Is that too much to ask?"

9: One hour fifty minutes after

Lacy and Sam are outside the mother's house, standing next to the car. "Sam. You have to drive," says Lacey.

"Me? I was the one who wanted to stay."

"You're the least fucked up. Can't expect either of us to drive after what we've been through."

"But I smoked some pot."

"That was an hour ago. Come on, Sam. Don't be a wuss."

"What are you doing out there!" yells Chloe inside the car. "Sam! Get in and drive!"

"Come on, Sam. You know this route. Better than me, by now."

"Guess I'm not too messed up," Sam mutters.

"Sam? Sam?" Chloe slaps the window with her hand.

"Stop wasting time, Sam. We need to get to I-5 before dark." Lacey climbs into the back seat.

"It's already dark." Sam sighs and gets behind the wheel.

"Sam, what were you doing out there?" Chloe asks.

"Nothing," Sam turns the ignition key.

"What were you two talking about?"

"Nothing," he replies.

"I heard you talk to each other."

"It was nothing, Chloe."

He backs out of the driveway. In minutes Lenox falls behind them. The road is dark and winding. Sam's hands tremble on the steering wheel. The road has deep trenches on the sides and no shoulders. A four-wheel pickup jacked on monster tires like what a redneck who just won the lottery would drive, tears past them and slowly vanishes as two red eyes into the night. Two large MAGA flags on the tailgate.

"Can you go any faster?" Lacey asks from the back seat.

"We'll get to the highway soon," Sam says.

"We've been on this road forever."

"Don't blame me!" he snaps. "We should have stayed. If you two hadn't . . ."

"Shut up, Sam," Chloe barks from the passenger seat. "Nothing we can do about that now."

"But is this the right thing?"

"What do you mean, Sam?"

"We should have stayed the night," he says.

Chloe doesn't answer. After a pause, Lacey leans towards the front. "We don't have options, Sam. We can't stay back there."

"But they'll want to talk to you and Chloe. You were witnesses. Explain to them what happened."

"Nothing to explain, Sam. No reason to stay."

"And you lied to your mom about the time. She wouldn't want us to drive this late."

"That wasn't me. Her clock was slow."

"Did you change it, Lacey?"

"Please, Sam," Chloe moans. "Can you be quiet for one damn minute?"

"But Chloe . . ."

"Shut up, Sam!" Her voice explodes in the car. Wincing, Sam almost swerves off the road. "You're making things worse!" she continues. "Everyone shut up!"

Everyone complies. Sam takes a deep breath and regains control of the car. He glances over. Chloe's hunched inside the hoodie, squeezed down in the seat. He's about to ask her if she's feeling okay, but the anger of her words cuts into him.

As he drives, he seethes. He doesn't know what is going on and they won't tell him. The pot and alcohol from earlier have worn off, to leave his mind numb and tired. The road is an endless ribbon through the forested slopes, the head beams marking out a tunnel of light in the dark forest chaos. Talking took his mind off the tedium of the drive, and now the silence in the car wraps over him, tightening around his skull.

Onward through the passing canopy of trees around one steep bend and another. The contortions of the road are hypnotic as if entering an endless tunnel. They should have reached the interstate by now. He begins to doubt he's on the right road.

10: Seven hours before

A couple dozen people are at the funeral. To Sam it is sad, but a bit absurd, a dead body in a fancy wooden box with the lid propped open for everyone to see, as if the father is asleep or in a trance. He has a contemptuously smug smile on his flabby face. After some time, the coffin is shut. Sam's mother-in-law insists he be a pallbearer because fat Cletus Scroggins might have a heart attack.

They lead the procession as they bring the casket up the hill and past the trees to the more private part of the cemetery. They set it on the device that lowers it into the earth. After it is lowered people come up front to say things. Mark, Chloe's older brother, rambles about how much his father meant to him. Older sister Marsha spews religious stuff in her slow, hushed voice. Their mother says something about the nice time they had dancing to Big Band when they were young. Someone says "Thank god he wasn't a Trumper" and a few people giggle while others glare. Sam looks over at Mark who is not amused. Neither Chloe nor Lacey come up to say anything.

Afterward, they gather at the reception room at the funeral parlor, where wine and snacks are served. "You wuss-ed out," Lacey whispers to Chloe.

"I didn't want to hurt mom."

Lacey shakes her head. "Mom. Where was she? Those times we needed her most."

"You don't really think? Mom? There was nothing she could do."

Mark walks up to them. At least he's in a dark three-piece, a little too tight on him, and not his NRA flack vest and MAGA hat. "Glad you girls showed up. Lacey, you look exactly the same."

"You're the same too," Lacey says but she's appalled at how ugly her older brother has become. Since his divorce Mark has let himself go, exploding out of the three piece like the Hulk gone south, with a long wispy gray tinge at the upper rim of his naked cranium, that makes him into some pathetic Bozo the Clown.

Lacey feels sorry for Mark. The bitterness of his life etched on his face. She hopes she doesn't look that way in fifteen years when she's his age.

"You staying out of trouble?" he asks.

"I try to."

"Hopefully Chloe is a good influence on you. Good seeing you."

"Good seeing you, too, big brother," Lacey says, aware she has nothing else to say to him.

Mark's best friend Zeke approaches, eyeing her. "Hi, Lacey! Remember me? You're all grown and prettier than ever."

"Thank you, Zeke," she murmurs. "You still a cop?"

"Still sheriff deputy. But when Joe retires . . ." He gives her the up and down. "Coming to the after-party? It's at my place."

"Perhaps." She shrugs.

He leans in to her. "I always thought you were hot, Lacey. Even when you were ten years old."

"Shut up, Zeke!" Mark groans. "Stop hitting on my sister."

Lacey glances around the room and spots Chloe talking to Mrs. Bancroft, their high school math teacher.

"You be there Lacy," Zeke calls after her. She feels his creepy eyes as she crosses the room to Chloe. No fucking chance, she thinks.

11: One hour twenty minutes after

Sitting in her armchair, Lacy's mother asks, "why is Chloe acting strange?"

"I don't know," Lacy says. "Did you ask her?"

"And why weren't you at Zeke's house for the party?"

"Isn't it enough all the shit we had to hear before they lowered the body? Fuck our dad!"

"Hush, Lacey!" Her mother is mortified. "No good comes of talking ill of the dead."

"But what about the ill of the living? We're supposed to shut up, not say the truth while he rots down there absolved of his crimes? How is that supposed to sit with us? Huh, mom?"

The mother's voice is high-pitched and whiny in a pained way. "Why do we have to bring any of this up now? These things can be talked about tomorrow. We need a break from the sorrow of today."

"Tatty-tatty-tatty-tatty," Chloe starts to intone from outside the screen door. "Tatty-tatty-tatty-tatty." Over and over, with little chokes and sobs.

"What's she raving about?" the mother asks.

"You know what we're talking about. Don't pretend you don't know. You were there."

"There was nothing I could do," the mother protests. "This is very unfair, Lacey. Look at the job you did seeing after Chloe."

"The praising of that scoundrel has made her this way," Chloe says.

"Your dad made a few mistakes, but look how it ended, him hollow and alone, with only Mark looking in on him. Then he and Mark fought over that MAGA crap. At least we can give Gerard credit for not following the Great Grifter."

"One good thing. He wasn't a fucking Trumper. That's supposed to erase the shit he put us through? The way he stole our childhoods from us."

"Hush, Lacey! You must bury the past and live in the present."

"And simply forget it happened?"

"Forgive and forget, Lacey. I had a much harder childhood than you, and yet I raised you all far better than my parents done me."

"Yeah, great job, mom. Mark is a QAnon crazy, Marsha a medicated zombie, Dick is dead and Chloe and me will be in therapy for life."

"We all make mistakes. Remember when you stole Chloe's boyfriend, how mad she got?"

"Please, mom. We were fucking kids when that happened. Chloe is sicker than a dog, and we need to get her back tonight. Sam pulls an early shift tomorrow."

"But it's so late," her mother protests.

"Not at all. It's only seven." Lacey gestures to the clock radio on the cocktail table at her mother's elbow. "Plenty of time before the woods get haunted." Their mother looks at the clock in surprise, she could have sworn it was later, but maybe the hour or two has dragged because she's tired of dealing with her daughters.

"Mark can drive you to Portland. He goes in both tomorrow and Monday. And Sam can drive home early tomorrow."

"We'd rather get Chloe in her own bed. I think she'll pull out of it in the morning."

"But you were barely here a day, and you've been gone so long. You can't up and leave so abruptly when you just arrived."

"I'll return, Mom. But we need to go."

"Sam, are you okay with this? Driving at this hour?"

Sam enterx from the back of the house with his and Chloe's suitcases. "I'm fine. Don't worry, Mrs. Emerald."

"But I do, to see Chloe in that state."

"She'll be fine. She needs rest in her own bed."

"Better she rests here. Instead of driving all that way."

"This is for the best." He looks out at Chloe past the screen door. "I'm sorry she's like this, Mrs. Emerald."

12: Three hours before

"Chloe? We're not going to the after-party?" Sam asks.

"With Zeke there? Who knows what other creeps will show up."

They are on the empty bleachers at the high school. Chloe and Lacey pass around a joint.

"Besides," Lacey adds. "The party is for Dad. Bad enough we had to sit through the funeral. Hearing them praise that monster."

"I know I shouldn't say it but I'm glad he's dead and buried," Chloe says.

"Me too. Let's visit his grave. Let him know what we think of him."

"Now?" Intrigued, Chloe ignores the joint in her fingers.

"No. Let's check out the glove shop first." Lacey gets up off the bleachers.

"The glove shop. Yes." Chloe says.

It is all the talk of town beside the new steakhouse, a store called Beauregard Petite's Glovery that only sold gloves, an oddity for a hick town like Lenox. Twenty minutes later, Chloe and Lacey gaze at the gloves arrayed in the front window.

Sam knows that after smoking the joint Chloe and her sister will be in there forever. He spies a couple tables next block, in front of a thrift store, with boxes of LPs and DVDs

"Chloe!" he calls to them as they walk to the door. The sisters turn. He points. "Meet you up there browsing records."

Chloe thumbs up. Sam walks to the corner.

"Hey, dude. You got a light?" asks a man seated near the corner on a bench. A fat cigar between his lips waggles up and down as he talks. He's got thick sideburns and a mullet, wearing a jean vest and chains dangling from his pants to secure his keys and wallet. Sam recognizes the man, the same one they saw the night before, crossing the street, the man named Spike.

"No." Sam shakes his head. "Don't smoke."

"No?"

"Least not tobacco."

"Just the good stuff. You all right, man." The man gives him a thumbs up. "I guess I do have a light." He pulls out a lighter and lights the cigar.

Sam walks to the tables of records. As he riffles through a box, he keeps an eye out for Chloe and her sister. He starts to read the back of an LP that looks interesting. When he glances up, Chloe and her sister are at the corner, arguing with Spike.

"I was asking your sister, Chloe. Wasn't talking to you."

"Spike, you're a loser. Frankly, you disgust us," Lacey says.

"You're pathetic, Spike," Chloe adds.

"Fuck you, Chloe. You and your snob sister think you're too good for this town? The both of you're rotten little shits. Get the fuck away from me before I beat some sense into both of you." He pulls his cigar out of his mouth and hurls it at them. The stub hits Lacey, a sputter of sparks. Both women gasp and rush across the street towards Sam.

"Come back here, you little cowards," Spike hurls at them.

"This town, same old shit," Lacey says. "Why do they let him harass people?"

"He should be in jail. Makes me sick to see him." Chloe is ashen.

"What's going on?" Sam asks, looking up from a crate of records.

"That guy." Lacey jabs a thumb over her shoulder. "Trouble. Let's get a drink."

13: One hour ten minutes after

"Why're Chloe and Sam outside? Why don't they come in?" Gladys Emerald tries to peer past the screen door from her recliner. Old swing plays on the stereo, soothing to Gladys, reminding her of better times when she was young and beautiful.

"Why do you have this shitty music on?" Lacey asks.

"You don't find it soothing?"

"No! It's Dad's music!"

"He was a different person when we first met," Gladys tells her daughter. "I can't erase I once loved him. And he was your father. Without him, you're nothing."

"Fuck Mom, you did the hard work on that one."

"Hush, Lacey! That language!"

"Fucking get over it, Mom."

"Are you girls on drugs? Is Chloe having a bad trip? Is she freaking out? Is that why she won't come in?"

"No, mom. We all react to death in different ways. This is her way to grieve, but Chloe will be fine after some rest."

"Yes, bring her in for rest."

"That's what I'm explaining to you . . ."

"Lacey! Watch out! Oh! Look what you did!"

"It's nothing, Mother." Lacey rights the six-inch square cocktail table and stoops down to pick up the clock.

"You girls always were clumsy."

Lacey carefully sets the clock back on the table, the clock obscured by her back. "Anyway, Mother, we leave tonight."

"Tonight? You can't leave tonight."

Lacey turns to her. "We have to. Sam has an emergency call, and for Chloe's sake we decided to go with him."

"Chloe is in no condition to travel. Have Sam bring her inside to rest. Mark can bring you and Chloe back Sunday or Monday. He goes to Salem on Monday, and a gun show in Vancouver on Sunday."

"No. We go with Sam."

"But it's so late."

"No, mother." Lacey points to the clock. "Ten after seven. We'll be at the freeway before dark, and then it doesn't matter."

Gladys scrutinizes the clock. She must have read the seven as a nine because she had thought a few minutes ago it was nine. She feels tired enough for nine, but maybe she's tired from the funeral. Only seven. No wonder Mark hasn't come by, as he planned after a short visit to his father in his resting ground.

She glances out at the two shadows against the screen mesh. A thought comes into her head. "Lacey!" she shouts to the back of the house where Lacey has gone to retrieve her suitcase.

"Yes, mother?"

"They're not out there smooching in the dark, are they? I can't see them that well."

"Don't know, mother."

"It's rude of them to stay out there. Sam!"

"I don't think he can hear you." Lacey enters the room. "Sam! Come in!"

14: One hour thirty minutes before

They are on the back deck of the dive bar, drinking beers.

"What do you think?" Chloe asks. She shows off the gloves she bought, white ones in silk. "They feel so nice. I barely feel like I'm wearing them." Lacey has a similar pair that are red.

"Sorry to change the subject, but does that piece of shit still live at the trailer?" Lacey asks.

"Yes. On Oak Street behind the cemetery," Chloe replies.

"Why don't they arrest him?"

"I think Zeke would if he had a reason," Chloe says. "I usually avoid that corner when I come here. I forgot today."

"So that's the guy you avoid," Sam says.

Chloe nods.

"What did he do?"

"It was a long time ago. I was home from college. He still lived with his parents."

"When the parents died, Spike couldn't keep the house," Lacey adds. "That's when he moved to the trailer."

"So, I went over." Chloe lowers her voice. "He tried to get me to drink this mixed drink, and I didn't like the taste, and he kept insisting, and I got suspicious he wanted to drug me. So I poured it in the sink when he wasn't looking."

"Seriously?" Sam gasps.

"It gets worse," Lacey says. "Tell him the rest."

"His parents were gone for the weekend. But his uncle came over. Creepy guy. I'm like why's he here, and he asks me if I want to have sex with both of them. They had it planned out while the parents were away."

Chloe pauses to sip her drink. "I knew I had to get out of there, but Spike kept pestering me to stay. The uncle finally told him to let me leave. And now Spike lives by himself. No uncle to tell him no."

"Did you tell your mom?" Sam asks.

"No. I was freaked out. And nothing happened."

"Mom wouldn't know how to handle it anyway," Lacey says. "She'd blame you for going there in the first place. And shit, not like he's the only creep in this town that would pull that sort of shit."

15: Twenty minutes after

The trail levels off and emerges from the woods. Lacey has the gun in front of her, holding it by the barrel in one hand and the stock in the other. She can feel the heat of the barrel through the glove.

The trail edges along the perimeter of the lot, towards a road a hundred yards away. In front of her is Spike's trailer. The yard is scrubby, overgrown with weeds. As she takes a dozen steps closer, she hears voices from inside, a woman moaning and screaming.

What the fuck! She freezes for a moment, and then she realizes. He's watching porn. She can see through the window at the end of the trailer, the back of his head and the images of flesh moving on the large TV in front of him.

Eww! This is close enough. She gives the gun a toss into a large clump of crabgrass and turns and runs back to the trail.

Chloe and Sam wait at the top of the trail. Lacey peels off her white gloves and carefully stuffs them in her purse. They follow the perimeter of the cemetery to the parking lot and walk back toward town.

"So that's it?" Sam breaks the silence.

"I guess so," Lacey says.

"And we go to the police?"

"No. Mother's house."

"But we should talk to the police."

Lacey shakes her head. "Not the police around here. That fucker Zeke, Mark's friend. He's deputy sheriff and he hates me."

"But he has to do his job. Why does he..?"

"Because I told him off. He wanted to fuck me and . . ."

"Will you stop talking about fucking, Lacey!" Chloe hisses. "And you, Sam? Why do you ask such stupid questions?"

Sam clams up. In several minutes they approach the sheriff's department, but a block away they turn off, to the road to their mother's. Lacey, a dozen steps ahead, enters the house.

Chloe freezes as she reaches the front door. "I can't go inside. Can't go in there." Creepy music oozes out past the doorway, and any closer she knows it will be strong enough to crawl under her skin. She already has too much to cope with. It makes her think of that monster buried in the ground, the same monster that climbed inside her and scrambled her thoughts. Through the mesh of the screen door, she sees her mother on her big chair, in harsh confrontation with Lacey.

"Why can't you go in, Chloe?" Sam asks, next to her.

"I don't know. Stay out here with me, Sam."

"You feel better?"

"A little. I need to be calm. Take deep breaths. One step at a time. Move forward so I don't fall back."

"That's right," Sam says. "We'll sleep this off here and tomorrow morning head home."

"I want to go home tonight. Lacey does too."

"I guess," Sam says. "If it wasn't so late."

"Not that late. And the highway'll be lit up like twilight."

"Maybe you're right." He takes a deep breath and they snuggle as they hold hands and look through the mesh to inside the house. "I'm here with you."

"I know, Sam. I'm sorry to put you through this."

"No. Not at all." They stand together and watch Lacey return to the front room with her suitcase. "So . . . What happened back there?"

Her body tenses out of the snuggle. Her hand squeezes tight around his. "Back where? What are you talking about?"

He's about to say, at the grave, but he notices Lacey beckoning them to go inside.

"They want us inside," he says.

"No, Sam. They want you. Go in. Grab our stuff. I'll be fine out here."

"Don't you want to say good-bye to your mother?"

"Sam!" Lacey yells.

"Go in there Sam. Leave me out here alone."

He opens the screen and steps into the room. He looks over his shoulder; she continues to stand and look into the house, as if she is an observer and they are on some grotesque stage made to look like a primitive television screen to the viewers outside.

"Sam, what's wrong with Chloe?" the mother asks. "Has she been hurt?"

"Sam, tell dear mother we head back tonight," Lacey says.

"Is this so, Sam?" the mother accuses.

"I guess. That's what Chloe wants."

"But there's something wrong with her. Why won't she come inside?"

"She'll be fine, Mom," Lacey replies. "Remember when she had these fits as a child, and it would pass when she stayed somewhere else. It's the damn music, reminds her of the old house."

"She has the nerve. I thought we'd relax, drink wine, and reminisce."

"I don't think anyone needs more to drink." Sam remarks and glances out at Chloe.

The mother continues to babble: "And airing out all this other stuff too. I'm on your side. I suffered too. I divorced him when I found out."

"But now you revere his death by listening to this music," Lacey retorts.

"Not revering him. I'm reliving the few good moments I had in my life, before he got weird, before you kids with your troubles and woes. Those few years when we were young, best years of my life."

"And it ended because of us?"

"No. Because of age. Something you and Chloe won't realize until it's too late. The body begins to thrum with aches and pains. Everything becomes more difficult as the pain magnifies and you realize your life can be over, like Gerard's. When you know that all you have is family. We are by blood what we are."

"Shut up, Mother! Enough of your platitudes! Family means nothing if you don't do it right. That man can fucking rot in hell, he lost the right to be my dad a long time ago."

"Why, Lacey!" The mother is stricken. "Let's talk about something more happy."

"We have to leave, mother. Sam, you got everything?"

"Sam," their mother pleads. "Talk sense in her. Leaving this late at night."

"It's only quarter after seven," Lacey replies. "Plenty of time to reach I-5 before dark. If we leave now."

"Yes, I guess we're leaving, Mrs. Emerald," Sam says.

"But won't Chloe come in. Chloe!"

Chloe remains outside the door. Her shape delineated in the screen mesh, a shadow standing there, and her mother cannot tell if she's looking inside, or turned away, looking down the drive to the scraggle of woods along the hillside across the street.

16: Twenty minutes before

They reach the cemetery. "So, we walk up there and do this," says Lacey. "Say the things we wanted to say at the service. This will be our service for dear old Dad."

Chloe puts a hand on Sam's shoulder. "I think we need to do this alone, Sam. You stay here, wait at that bench. And be our lookout."

"Sure, if you give me the pot. It's after six so I can smoke some."

"Of course." She pulls the tin from her purse, extracts a joint and the lighter, and sticks the tin back in her purse.

She and Lacey start up the hill towards the grave site. Sam sits on the bench at the edge of the parking lot and watches them vanish past the shrubbery into the cemetery.

He takes a couple hits from the joint. Might as well get stoned, he thinks, since they will not be driving back tonight, already getting too late for that. The trip so far has been mostly drama-free, and his fear that Chloe would get into one of her moods like she usually does when she visits Lenox, has mostly dispelled. Even her reaction to that loser Spike hasn't changed that.

He takes a deep breath. The town is hidden behind a thicket of woods, though he can make out the roofs of the bank and the church over the tops of trees. He connects his earbuds to his phone to listen to music. Music always sounds better when high.

He starts to pull the LPs out of his shopping bag, reading the liner notes to one, looking at the cover, which is not in great shape, worn and peeling in places. He re-lights the joint to take another hit, cupping the flame from the breeze. Between a break in the music, he hears car tires on the dirt road, and he glances over. At the other end of the parking lot, a large pickup truck enters.

He drops the joint on the ground, pretends to look straight ahead while out of the corner of his eye, the truck pulls into place and a man gets out from the driver's side. Sam glances up to see Mark, Chloe's older brother, who ignores him. Mark has changed out of his black suit and is now in black jeans and a camo vest. At least he's not wearing his red MAGA cap, Sam thinks.

He's intimidated by Mark, but now Mark lacks his usual swagger, loping up the trail hesitantly. Is Mark part of the ceremony they planned which they wanted to leave Sam out of? Should he run up after Mark? Undecided, he remains on the bench. He picks up the half-finished joint and fires it up. He turns the music up louder.

17: Ten minutes after

Lacey and Chloe are in the cemetery, about seventy-five yards from their father's grave.

"No!" Lacey says. "Let me pick it up because I'm wearing gloves." She daintily plucks the cigar butt off the ground between her thumb and middle finger.

"Where is Sam? Why isn't he here?"

"I don't know, Chloe."

"Where are we going?"

"This way."

"We should look for Sam."

"We will, Chloe."

"Why are we going down here? I don't like this trail." She remembers the trail leads to the bottom of a hill at the back of Spike's trailer.

"I understand. We won't go down the trail. I'll leave his cigar there." Lacey drops the cigar on the edge of the trail, ten feet in from the graveyard.

"Leave it there?" Chloe asks.

"Yes. Now we find Sam. Over there. I think I see him."

"Sam?" Chloe strains to see across the way towards the parking lot, and a shape makes its way towards the main part of the cemetery. "Sam! We're over here!"

Sam turns and starts towards them.

"What's going on?" Sam shouts as he gets closer.

"Nothing, Sam. Will you stay here with Chloe?"

"Chloe?" Sam steps closer. "Chloe, are you okay?"

"I don't know!" she cries out.

"Back in a moment," Lacey spits out as she heads into the cemetery.

Chloe starts to tremble. "Where's Lacey going?"

"Up there. She'll be back. What happened?"

"I don't know. Sam, please hold me."

"There," he says, wrapping his body around hers. He pats her back as he hugs her. Maybe that's all she needs. "Take some deep breaths. We'll get through this."

"I hope so, Sam. You're so sweet."

"Did Mark do something?"

"Mark? What about Mark? Do you know about Mark?"

"Did he say something?"

"I don't know! Why do you keep saying his name?"

"Hey!" Lacey shouts as she hurries towards them, holding something in front of her in her gloved hands. "Don't make so much noise, you love birds."

As she gets closer, Sam sees that she has a revolver, holding it with the thumb and forefinger of both hands, by the barrel and the back of the handle, like a very fat rat too heavy to hold in one hand.

"Lacey?" Sam stares at her. "What's going on? Is that Mark's gun?"

"Will you stay calm? You're upsetting Chloe." She paces past him and her sister.

"Where're you going?" he asks.

"I'll be back."

"Lacey, wait for me." Chloe turns and follows from twenty feet behind. Sam watches them leave as he tries to gather his thoughts. Something is going on, and no one will tell him a thing. He hurries after them.

Chloe stands at the edge of a trail. Lacey, further on, makes her way down the hill until she vanishes beyond the wooded shrubs.

"We're not going down?" he asks.

"No. I can't."

"Why not?"

"He.." She chokes up in fear.

"The guy on the corner with the cigar," he remembers. "Spike." Chloe flinches at the mention of his name. Sam takes a deep breath. "Did he do something?"

"I . . . I don't know, Sam. I can't tell you."

"What is it, you don't know or you can't tell?"

"Sam, why are you acting so mean?"

"Not trying to be mean, I was trying to . . ." fuck it. He clamps his lips tight. In a few minutes Lacey re-appears on the trail, no longer holding the gun.

18: Fifteen minutes before

Lacey and Chloe walk hand in hand, towards the fresh grave. Lacey digs into her pocket. Grabs something she doesn't recognize and pulls it out. "Eww!" She shakes it out of the hankie and it falls to the ground.

"What is it?" Chloe asks, stooping to look.

"Some weird bug must have jumped in my pocket."

"No, it's that asshole's cigar. When he threw it at us."

"Ugh!" Lacey cringes. She grabs Chloe's hand again. They continue towards the grave, a hundred steps further.

"You know what would be funny?" Chloe says. "If we pissed on his grave."

19: One minute after

The gun lies on the ground, a dozen feet from the grave site.

"Chloe, what just happened? Fuck!"

Chloe backs away, her eyes shut. "Lacey, I'm scared. Help me, Lacey."

"It's okay Chloe. Deep breaths."

"Lacey, help!"

"We need to keep walking. Get away from here."

Lacey guides Chloe away from the grave. Chloe clutches to her in desperation, eyes shut. After a dozen steps, Chloe flutters her eyes open.

"My hands!" Chloe pulls off the new gloves and puts them in her jacket pocket. "They were crushing my hands. Is . . . is Mark okay?"

"I don't know. I think he'll be okay."

"I can't remember what happened."

"Don't try to remember," Lacey says. "Not yet. We can sort this out. We need to stay calm. We need to take a deep breathe, and tell ourselves. Everything will be okay." But Lacey is not convinced as she glances around in fear. If they call the sheriff, they will have to deal with Zeke, and neither she nor Chloe want that. What would the sheriff's department say anyway? Could they prove it was an accident? And Chloe is freaking out, as she clutches at Lacey and they step through the graveyard.

"Chloe, you have to pull yourself together!"

"What happened? Is Mark okay?"

"I don't know, Chloe. This isn't good, but we can't lose our heads."

"What are we to do?"

"Need to stay calm."

"I don't even know what happened."

"It was an accident, Chloe."

"An accident. But what happened?"

"No one's fault, Chloe. An accident."

"Is Mark okay?"

"I don't know. Let me think." Lacey scans desperately everywhere looking and thinking as panic thunders through her veins. Her eyes fix on an object on the ground, a cigar butt, the one she found in her pocket several minutes earlier. Spike's cigar. All at once she has a vision.

"Is Mark okay?" Chloe asks again.

"I don't know. But there's our answer." Lacey stops in her tracks. Chloe follows Lacey's finger to the cigar. She freezes in fear.

"Spike? Is Spike here?"

"Doesn't matter, Chloe. There's work to do before we call anyone."

20: Grave incident

Mark trudges slowly through the cemetery towards his father. He wants a moment to be alone with the grave, to talk to his father, to apologize to his father for being angry at their disagreements. As he gets closer he notices his two sisters, Chloe and Lacey. Good, they've finally come to their senses, he thinks as he lopes nearer. Their backs to him, they don't see him. But what are they doing squatting like that above the freshly-turned dirt? Their voices trickle into his ears, laughter, and . . .

Mark steps closer in horror . . . The evil! Mark sees red as he rushes towards them. Urinating on father's grave! How could they! Lacey must have put Chloe up to it.

"Let go of her!" Chloe shrieks.

"You . . . you monster!" Mark screams in Lacey's face. He clutches her arms to her sides. "And you put your sister up to this shit!"

"Let go! You're hurting me!"

"Stop it! Get off her!" Chloe yells.

In a wildfire of rage, Mark shakes Lacey like a rag doll. He's suddenly aware of a tug on his belt as the gun slides free of the holster.

"Stop that!" He lets go of Lacey in panic. Chloe pulls loose the gun. "What are you..? Don't touch that!" He grabs at her hand and the gun explodes, the sound deafening. All three siblings freeze at the sound. Lacey in front of him is in shock, and Chloe, at an angle, and slightly nearer, looks confused as they both stare at him.

At first he thinks one of them got hit, perhaps Lacey with that surprised look on her face, but she remains standing. He glances down past her neck, the light jacket and jeans, but sees no sign of a wound. Chloe too remains standing, her eyes shut, face squeezed tight, He has an odd feeling as a dull ache creeps up his chest. He looks down. A hole in his camo vest. Blood pulses out, and dribbles down his belly to his thigh. Dizzy and light-headed, he is not sure what will happen next, but the rage has vanished, replaced by an intense fear. His two sisters blur in his vision as everything becomes shades of red. They step away as he stumbles and falls, unable to stop himself as his father's grave rushes up to greet his face.

Q d'ETAT

1

As they get close to downtown, they drive past the shortcut without veering off. "Brock?" Ange asks her brother. "Aren't we going to Dad's?"

"No, headed to the hardware store." Brock continues to look ahead as he steers the pickup truck. "Then I'll take you home."

"Hardware store? I don't need anything."

"I need to run in," he says.

"You couldn't drop me off first?" she suggests, slightly annoyed. "And I'm picking up Chad."

"So?"

"You need a new boyfriend, Ange."

Brock's best friend Chad, who owns the hardware store? Ange gags. "Don't need your help, Brock." She's twenty-four years old and her older brother still treats her like a kid.

"The right person for you. Lots of people, they don't know what's going down." He glances over at her as they wait for the light to change.

"Like those crazies, downtown?" she asks.

"Like that kid the other day," he grunts, stepping on the gas..

"What kid?" She feigns confusion.

"That kid." Brock glances at her. "Leaving Dad's house a few days ago?"

"Oh, him. Ethan. He's a friend from the U."

"Keep it that way, Ange. You need a real man. Not some kid from the university."

"I don't want to hear it, okay? And Ethan's just a friend."

"Be careful. I don't want you hurt. When the civil war breaks out . . ."

"I won't get hurt," she says. "I carry around that can of mace you got me."

"You should get a handgun, Ange. Those people at the University are brainwashed."

She doesn't respond. Why the fuck can't he take her home first? He is tense, fingers rigid on the steering wheel, lips twisted in a tight grin that stretches his face taut. He's in another world she wants no part of. She stares out the side window at the houses and businesses and apartments as downtown looms closer.

The car radio buzzes with news about the pending results of the election from the previous day, and the contested ballots in half a dozen states, including theirs. Protesters are outside the county election office of their city. Brock switches to Freedom Radio. The talk host claims no one knows where many of the votes came from, implying illegal votes poured in at the last moment to change the results. The host tells the listeners they can't let this happen again.

"We must stop the steal now. Never again! Haven't they persecuted this great American enough? Is this how we treat success? Take arms now! We can't wait for another January sixth."

How can they air such lies, she wonders, hating the broadcast but not quite brave enough to change the station or turn it off, or argue with her brother about it. And how can Brock, three years older than her, take all that bullshit seriously?

They pull into a space across the street from the hardware store. Ange waits for Brock to go inside. She climbs out of the truck to walk home.

2

Chad's blood pressure flares up. The talk radio is disturbing: the most important election of their lifetime on a razor margin, as the talk host mentions several times. The other side wants to steal it like they did before. Everything Troy said seems clear. This is their last chance to save America, stop the steal, and fight against the big lie.

Chad listens to Freedom Radio during his lunch half-hour, but he switches back to classic rock when he flips the sign to OPEN. A customer is a customer, and politics are offensive to some. He can't risk losing business from snowflake college kids because they can't handle the truth. His one concession to politics is the Q-Anon sticker, a red "Q," on his front window.

A man in his forties, trim build, receding hairline, walks into the store, grabs a pack of batteries, and pushes them onto the counter. Chad rings him up and runs his credit card.

"I noticed the Q outside," says the man.

"Q?"

"The Q. On your window." The man points to the window by the door with the sticker.

Chad narrows his eyes slightly. "What of it?"

"It's brave of you to put that up."

"Really?"

"Yeah."

"Where we go one we go all." Chad hands back the credit card.

"There are a lot of haters in this town," says the man. "So I appreciate you doing this."

Chad grins. "You got that. But what can you do? I know that sticker might upset some people, but I know right from wrong." He looks at the man's name on the computer screen. "Can I call you Jerry?"

"Sure thing."

"I'm Chad."

"I'm new to town, Chad, and my stuck friends don't know anything. You know, a place to meet other people like you and I."

Chad leans over the counter and lowers his voice. "Other Qs?"

"Yes. Qs." Jerry smiles.

Chad grabs a card from the stack at the back of the register and slides it across the counter. "Here's where some of us go. Good place. Strong drinks. If you know the right people, Jerry."

"Thank you," says Jerry as he glances around. "Got a nice store here."

"I hope so."

"I'm headed down to the elections with some friends," Jerry says.

"You are? Me too. Closing for the day as soon as my pal gets here."

"Hope we don't have a stolen election."

"You got that, man! Not again. Maybe I'll see you down there. We need numbers. Make sure this vote doesn't sour."

"Phone ringing. Need to get this." Jerry steps quickly outside the door and puts the cellphone to his ear.

Chad watches him depart. Good to see a man who knows what's happening, who sees past the facade of Lame Stream News, to the truth. They have to stop another election steal. Troy Majors said they need more recruits, with the protests threatening to erupt into riots that will unleash an Antifa doomsday on downtown. Chad worries the riots will spread further; his store is only seven blocks from the election offices.

Brock bursts into the store and steps up to the counter.

"Hi, Chad. I have to take Ange home before we meet the others."

"Sure, Brock."

"And you'll sit next to her? Sweet talk her?"

Chad glances up from the register, which he has set to print the daily totals. "I don't think she cares about me, to be honest."

"Keep trying. I think she's warming to you. A successful business-man like you? Compared with that over-aged school kid she's seeing?"

Brock steps behind the counter, and pulls out the box with the Hawaiian shirts and their MAGA hats. "You always liked her, Chad."

"You got mad at me for that."

"That was before. Now with the world so dangerous, so many leftist crazies out there, she needs someone to keep her on our side. I don't want her brainwashed by those woke communist extremists at the university."

"You really think your sister'd fall for that crap?" Chad asks.

3

Stepping out of the hardware store, Jerry stops to reflect. He now has batteries to his cam backup and a new friend. He can't wait to tell Ethan and the others. The small pink Q on the window is a brave act with all the right-wingers arriving into town to disrupt the elections, roaming the streets for gays to beat up. The extreme right could target the store and then what? A rock in the window would be the least problem. Arson? Looting? Chad is taking a risk.

Chad even gave Jerry a card to a gay bar. The town is dangerous, every toxic incel piece-of-shit trying to impress the Proud Boy brown shirts by beating up a gay or hippy for points. The queers needed a secret code word, so they called themselves by "Q," or so Jerry surmises.

Outside the hardware store, Jerry texts Ethan while a large black pickup truck parks across the street. A man steps out, slams the door. In a sleeveless gray tee and tight black jeans, he has a bit of flab in the stomach, but Jerry admires the arms and the biceps as the man walks towards him.

The man nods to him before entering the store. The passenger side door of the pickup truck opens and slams. A woman in jeans and tee emerges, walking up the street. She raises her hand to wave at someone beyond Jerry's view. Jerry's phone tings again.

"Hello, Ethan."

"Where you at?" Ethan asks.

"I'm outside a hardware store on Ash."

"Hey. I spotted someone I know. Hold on."

Jerry walks down the steps to the sidewalk. Up the street, the woman approaches a bus stop kiosk.

"I'm back," Ethan says. "Where did you say you were?"

"Ash Street. Between Fifth and Sixth," Jerry says.

"I'm real close. Bus stop at Sixth."

"I see you!" Jerry exclaims. Half a block away, at the edge of the bus stop, Ethan is face to face with the woman. Ethan looks over her shoulder, and she turns to look too.

"Ethan!"

"Jerry!" Ethan waves.

"What?" Jerry yells back, approaching.

"Come meet my friend."

The woman is young, with startling green eyes and dark hair. This must be the one Ethan told Jerry about last night when they went out for drinks after Jerry arrived at the airport.

"Jerry, my friend Ange." Ethan beams. "I told her we're headed to the protest."

"Not sure I want to go," she says.

"Why not?" Jerry asks. They begin to head away from the hardware store.

"Won't it be dangerous?"

"Ange has never done a protest," Ethan adds.

"It won't be dangerous," Jerry says. "We'll keep our distance from the troublemakers."

"That's what I told her." Ethan looks at her. "Just come along, and if you don't like it, I'll walk you home."

"I guess, if it's okay to tag along." She glances at Jerry.

"Sure," Jerry says. "More the merrier." He turns to Ethan. "I just chatted with the owner of the hardware store back there. Nice guy."

"Chad?" Ange gasps.

"That's right. You know him?"

"Not really. Friend of my brother."

"Small world. We might see him down there." Jerry looks back and points. "I think that's him over there."

The man from the pickup truck and Chad are three blocks away, too far to make out clearly. Their colorful shirts are visible even at a distance. They pause in the middle of the street as if gazing back at Jerry, Ethan, and Ange.

Ethan glances up from his phone. "Latifa and Suzy are here. One street over this way." He points to the cross street. "Let's go."

4

"Where the hell did she go?" Brock stops in the middle of the street. Ange is not in the truck.

"Who?" Chad asks. He steps out and looks too. They have changed into bright Hawaiian shirts and red MAGA caps.

"My sister. She vanished." Brock sends her a quick text.

"Maybe she walked home," Chad says.

"I hope so." Brock glances down the street. In the distance are three people, but they are too far away to make out details. He squints his eyes, wondering if one of the blurs is Ange. "I don't want her downtown with what might go down."

"She hates politics." Chad says. "She won't go downtown."

"Yeah. Maybe you're right." Brock walks towards the truck.

"Need to lock up and then I'll join you." Chad heads back to the store.

Brock climbs in behind the wheel and looks at his phone. Ange hasn't texted back. Chad climbs in the passenger side and Brock starts the vehicle.

"You nervous?" Chad asks.

"Nervous? Not really. More anxious."

"It might get ugly down there."

"I'm sure it will. That's why we have to be down there. You ready?"

"I think so, Brock."

Another three blocks, into the back lot of an old brick warehouse, they pull up next to Troy Major's panel van, its back doors open. Troy and Zack, in Hawaiian shirts and red MAGA caps, wait outside the van. Troy brushes his fingers across his immaculately trimmed beard while his thuggish nephew Zack, towering over him, has mouth agape.

"We're the first ones here besides Troy," Brock remarks.

5

"Ethan?" Ange whispers, clutching his hand. Jerry is several feet ahead of them.

"What is it, Ange?"

"I don't mind going to the protest, but I don't want to hang out with my brother and Chad."

"Chad?" Ethan asks.

"Hardware store. Jerry thinks he's a nice guy."

"We don't need to. Plenty of other people there. It'll be fun."

"I hope so. I think people should stay away, let those people at the election office do their jobs."

"That's why we're going. To counter the people trying to stop the elections. Jerry plans to film it."

"You think you can stop them?" she asks.

"Not sure. But I do what I can. I'm scared what might happen to this country."

"I see that. Do you think it makes a difference? To go down and protest?" Ethan sighs. "I don't know. It makes me feel better."

Ange's phone tings. Another text from her brother, but she doesn't want to answer. Ethan points up the street. "Wait 'til you meet our other friends, Latifa and Suzy."

Up ahead, two women in black hoodies stand at the corner. One raises her voice. "Jerry! You're in town!" Jerry greets them with big hugs while Ethan and Ange approach. One woman is black, with short-cropped hair that reminds Ange of Grace Jones. The other has long blond hair and very blue eyes.

"Latifa! Suzy!" Ethan calls out. "Meet my friend, Ange."

The women smile. "Hi, Ange," says the black woman. "I'm Latifa and this is Suzy."

"Nice meeting you, Ange," Suzy says, looking from her to Ethan.

The black woman is familiar and her name triggers a memory: the living room, Ange's brother and his cohort yelling names at a grainy video on the TV of a woman at an outdoor podium. Ange could not understand why they reviled the woman when they couldn't hear what she said over their yelling.

"You're the one in the video," Ange blurts nervously. "Antifa Latifa."

Latifa grimaces. "Some call me that after Randy Know stuck that label on me."

"Randy Know is an utter creep," Ethan mutters. "A propagandist for Fascism. None of those people know the difference between Antifa and BLM, and other protesters."

"As if anyone could be an Antifa leader," Jerry adds with a chuckle.

"Ange, my friends call me Latifa."

Ange nods. "Okay, Latifa."

They begin to walk towards the county elections office near the center of town. Ange glances over at Latifa and Suzy again, and then at Jerry, who now has a small film camera in his hand, which he pulled out of his backpack. None of them seem to be armed. She pulls on Ethan's arm, to indicate for him to slow down.

"Ange?" he says. "What's wrong?"

"I'm just nervous."

"Nervous, why?"

"Latifa."

"Latifa makes you nervous?"

"No, but some people want to hurt her."

He shrugs. "Unfortunately."

"People with guns. My brother hangs out with some of them."

"Your brother?" Ethan asks.

She nods her head. "They hate her. I don't think my brother would do anything, but some of his asshole friends . . . Isn't she scared?"

"I'm sure she is. But she won't let that stop her."

"Will Antifa be there?" she asks.

"I think so. That okay?"

"I don't know. Are they any better than the right-wing extremists? Using violence?"

"I guess they think so. Fight fire with fire. And they only use violence against fascists."

"Sure," she says. "Anti-fascist is what Antifa stands for. Antifa started as resistance to Mussolini. But did it do any good? Mussolini still rose to power, and then we got Hitler and Franco. And when Antifa commits violence, it strengthens the hands of the enemy. An excuse to create a bigger police state. Antifa provides ammunition for right-wing extremists, who try to link them with the people who want progress."

"Someone needs to stand up against Fascists," he replies. "If everyone remains complacent, and no one resists? If not Antifa, who?"

6

"Does anyone need a mask?" Latifa calls out.

"Masks?" Ethan and Ange ask in unison.

"Yes." Latefa pulls some Mardi Gras masks out of her purse. "To add to the festivities."

"Not me." Jerry waves his camera. "I'm on work hours."

"I'll take one," Ange says. She grabs a pink. Suzy takes a blue, and the other two are both pink as well.

"You want one, Ethan?"

"I don't know." Ethan points. "The costume store is here. Maybe I'll get one I really like."

"Ethan doesn't want pink." Suzy chuckles. "It's only conditioning that pink is seen as effeminate. Before the 1950s, pink was for boys and girls alike."

"You do what you need to do, Ethan," Latifa says.

"Just be a minute." Ethan turns and enters the costume shop. Ange thinks about going in after him but decides to talk to the others instead.

"I swear, straight guys," Latifa remarks with a roll of her eyes before she excuses herself and follows Ethan inside.

"How do you know Ethan?" Suzy asks Ange.

"I do admin for the History Department at the U," she replies. "And Ethan's working on his masters, so he comes into the office from time to time."

"He needs to get that thing done," Jerry groans. "He's almost thirty."

"Tell me about it," Ange says. "Says he'll have it done by the end of the year. And then he'll need to make a big decision." As she speaks, her eyes focus on a man halfway up the street headed in a fast walk towards them. Is that Chad? "What's he doing here?" "What's that?" Jerry and Suzy turn to follow her gaze. Chad is near. He calls out to Jerry. Jerry calls back. Chad spots her and pauses, recognizes her, in spite of the mask. "My best friend's little sister," he says as he leers at her. The others smile and nod. Chad's boots clatter across the porch and he's inside the store. Ange gasps for breath.

"That's the hardware store guy," Jerry tells Suzy. "I had a nice talk with him."

"And he's related to you, Ange?"

"No. He's my brother's friend."

"I take it you don't think much of him," Suzy says.

"You take it right."

"Why?" Jerry asks.

Ange shrugs. "Much as I love my brother, I don't want to know what him and his friends are up to." As if noticing her discomfort, Suzy and Jerry change the subject to the elections.

Latifa steps outside. "He's almost done. But you look troubled, Ange."

"It's nothing, Latifa."

"This is Ange's first protest," Jerry says. "Isn't that right?"

Ange nods.

"It won't be dangerous if enough of us are there," Latifa says. "People like you, Ange, willing to stand up for what is right."

Ange hasn't thought of it that way before, to be part of something, to bring about change for the better, when these last several years the world has ratcheted the other way.

7

In the parking lot behind the warehouse, the men wait for others to arrive.

"Okay, here's the plan," Troy says. "Brock, you and Chad are cover. You're setting off smoke bombs."

"Is this legal?" Chad asks.

"Of course. They are not dangerous. And no one will know who you are."

"Come on, Chad," Brock says. "No big deal. We're not doing anything wrong. We're patriots."

Troy adds, "when you have justice on your side . . . And we won't have justice on our side if this election goes bad. We're in a fight to save this country."

"It's a precaution, Chad," Brock says. "In case anything goes wrong. Merely a precaution."

"A percussion! That's what it will be." Zack chuckles. "A percussion grenade."

"If you say so, Brock." Chad trusts Brock far more than Troy or Zack.

"This is how it will go down," Troy tells them. "An explosive device goes off near the elections, and a riot starts. That's all the state legislature need and my guy inside thinks it's a done deal. The vote counts stopped, the legislators decide the election, our guy wins the state and Antifa gets blamed for the riot. And as a bonus, we put some of that scum in jail."

"Yeah!" Zack grunts. "Maybe they throw Auntie Fa-teeth-ah in jail."

"How do you know they'll set off bombs?" Chad asks.

"They will." Troy gives him an imperious stare. "Antifa thugs will do anything to cause violence and destruction."

"You still need to get a mask, Chad," Brock says.

"A mask?"

"Yes." Troy glares. "We're infiltrating Antifa. You need a mask."

"Chad, I thought I told you . . ." Brock adds, exasperated, as he reaches into the back of his truck.

"I . . . I assumed it was optional." Chad looks at the others nervously.

"You need one like this." Troy holds up the mask, a silver mirrored surface, faceless. Brock's mask is similar.

"That costume shop on Maple will have them." Brock points down the street.

"We can wait," Troy says. "The others aren't here yet. Go!"

Chad walks rapidly towards the costume shop. He remembers the shelf with those masks at the store. Brock told him to get one, but he forgot. He hopes the others aren't upset at his faux pas. Feeling conspicuous wearing the MAGA cap without the others around, he pulls it off and stuffs it in his back pocket without breaking stride.

He's not clear on the plans, and he is anxious at what is to come. The most important election of their lifetime. Perhaps their last chance to prevent socialism from weakening the nation. There was no end to how far the enemy will go, from the mock trials and impeachments to the blatant lies everyday on lame-stream news. Now their Antifa minions plot to bomb the elections? Is there no low to which left-wing extremists will go?

The costume shop is up ahead. He notices some people outside. Two women with masks over their eyes and . . . He recognizes the man.

"Jerry?"

"Hi, Chad," Jerry smiles. "These are some friends of mine. Ange and Suzy."

The woman in the pink mask scowls at Chad.

"I know her." Chad points to Ange. "She's my friend's little sister. Nice meeting you guys, but no time to talk. Got people waiting."

Chad enters the store. At least Brock will be relieved that Ange is with Jerry and not the liberal freaks from the university. Once Chad has the mask, he can join Jerry and the two women and head back down with them. Get closer to Ange, unless she and Jerry are with each other. The blonde woman is attractive too. Maybe the four of them can double-date later.

Inside the store, Chad races down the aisle to the mirror-masks. A man hovers over the shelf, which is bereft of inventory. The man ignores a single silver mask in front of him as he glances up and down the depleted shelves.

Chad slows as he comes closer. The man stares at the mask.

"Excuse me." Chad reaches across the space in front of the man. The man grabs hold of the mask at the same time Chad does.

"Seriously? I was here first." The man stares at Chad, a pleading look on his face.

"I didn't know you wanted it. You were standing there not doing anything."

"I do want it. I was here first."

"They probably have more in the back room," Chad reasons. "You didn't make a decision until I grabbed it. Let me have this one, I'm in a hurry. C'mon. I came for this specific mask."

"But I grabbed it first."

Neither of them lets go. They hold the mask between them and glare at each other. Though slightly larger than Chad, the man looks soft and

Chad thinks he can take the man in a fight, but not without risking the mask being torn.

"Just let go."

"Ethan? What the hell?" A black woman in a hoodie appears from around the corner.

"I saw this mask and this guy . . ."

"Not that one, Ethan. The ones over there, that just go over the eyes."

"Fine." The man lets go. Chad breathes a sigh of relief and takes the mask to the front counter.

Chad steps outside with the mask. The black woman has joined Jerry, Ange, and the blonde, Sally or Suzy.

"Hey, Chad." Jerry waves him over. "Come meet another friend of mine."

The black woman is familiar, Chad thinks, as he approaches, squinting against the sunlight. It can't be.

"This is Latifa," Jerry says.

The name sets off alarm bells. Identity confirmed. Antifa Latifa! Chad almost drops the mask. "She's . . . I need to . . ." He stammers, trying to make sense of things as he stares at Jerry and reels backward away from them.

"What's wrong, Chad?"

Chad points a finger. "She's a terrorist! One of the leaders!"

"No, she's not. That's absurd." Jerry smiles.

"Yes, she is!"

"She's queer, like you and me."

"Queer? Who the fuck . . ." Chad stares at Jerry's face, to find some sign of a joke.

The door to the shop opens and out steps the man who tried to grab Chad's mask. The man freezes. The door shuts behind him. "What's going on? Jerry? Latifa?" His eyes fix on Chad. "You got your damn mask."

"Ange! Come with me!" Chad pleads.

"No," she snaps. "I'm with my friends."

"They're not friends. They're troublemakers. Jerry, I thought you were part of Q."

"Q-Anon?" the other man sputters. "No way! Jerry'd never . . ."

Appalled, Chad focuses on Ange. "Ange, come here!"

"I don't have to listen to you."

"Your brother will be upset."

"I don't give a fuck," she says. "He doesn't own me. I'm twenty-four years old."

"You need to buzz off, tough boy," Antifa Latifa growls.

Chad glares at them, but what can he do? They outnumber him. Fortunately, none of them has drawn a weapon, since he's unarmed. Nothing to do but back away as quick as he can. Antifa Latifa, less than a dozen feet away from him. Jerry's betrayal punches him in the gut. And Ange, telling him off to be with these monsters.

Chad's finally far enough that he dares to turn his back on them. He needs to tell the others. As he scurries he pulls out his phone. But what to say? Jerry's betrayal has him worried. He recalls his conversation with Jerry in the store. Is that even the man's real name? How could Chad be so blind? The man faked friendship with him, to get info on the Q-Anon network. A spy, working closely with Antifa Latifa. How much information did Chad divulge? He even gave the man a card to the tavern where the Q crowd, the valiant few, met.

If Troy Majors finds out, he'll be furious with Chad. Better to talk to Brock. Brock answers on the first ring.

"Where the hell are you?"

"A block away. Listen, Brock . . ."

"Just get here, okay. Everyone's ready to go." Brock hangs up.

Chad rounds the corner into the lot behind the warehouse. Several other men, the rest of Troy's circle, are there, in Hawaiian shirts and red MAGA caps. Troy, Zack, and Brock have pulled black hoodies over their own shirts, and they glance over at him with their faceless mirrored masks.

"What took you so long?" Troy asks.

"I . . . I saw Antifa Latifa."

"Really?" Brock's voice booms from another mask.

"Yes. Back there. Near the costume store."

"And you didn't pull a citizen's arrest?" Troy, indignant.

"I was unarmed. Couldn't do a thing."

"If I saw Antie Fala-teeth-a. I woulda fuck that bitch up." Zack brags loudly.

Troy shakes his masked head. "These are dangerous times. Praise the Lord you're okay, Chad, but you boys need to be armed at all times. Especially when shit is hitting the fan. If I'd known I would have brought extra weapons."

Troy probably sleeps with an AK-47, Chad thinks to himself. "Maybe we can go back and catch her," Chad says aloud.

A few of the men say "yeah!" Zack shouts it gleefully.

"Pull a citizen's arrest? Tempting," Troy surmises. "But she's headed same place as use. We need to stick with the mission." Troy digs into a duffelbag. "Chad, you need this too." He tosses a hoodie. Chad catches it. A cheap over-sized one Troy probably bought at Walmart like those worn by Troy, Brock, and Zack to hide their brightly colored shirts.

"Me, Zack, Brock, and Chad will infiltrate Antifa," Troy says. "Rest of you will stand down unless fighting breaks out. When we give the signal, when the explosion is about to go off, you two set off the smoke bombs." He gestures to Brock and Chad. "Pull the pin and drop it on the ground. We ditch the hoodies and join the rest of our guys." Troy points to a pudgy dark-complexioned man with a backpack and a camera. "Randy Know here will document it all, catching Antifa in another act of willful destruction and violence to interfere with democracy and freedom."

Chad and Brock each tuck a smoke bomb into the front pocket of their hoodies. Zack has a messenger bag on a shoulder strap. Troy shuts the back of the van. "We'll see the rest of you down there."

Randy Know and the other group head around to the front of the building while Chad follows Troy, Zack, and Brock down a narrow alley to the next street.

"You guys stay here," Troy says. He steps out onto the side street and walks towards the end.

"Brock?"

"What is it?" Brock turns his masked face towards Chad.

"How do we know Antifa will set off a bomb?"

"Troy got info on it."

"That's right," Zack snickers. "Bombs. Someone will set a bomb alright."

"Is that what you have in the bag, Zack?" Chad asks. He had briefly seen Troy put an explosive device in Zack's bag, and it did not look like a smoke bomb.

"Listen, Chad, it's nothing," Brock says. "A percussion grenade. Loud bang, no one gets hurt."

"Going to be fun!" Zack hoots.

"Why do we need it if Antifa are setting off a bomb?" Chad asks.

"First, do we know for sure they will? Second, they set off a real bomb, people get hurt. We'll preempt that from happening. Once the riot begins, the police will be there with snipers, in case they do break out a bomb or two."

"It'll be hell down there," Chad remarks.

"You better believe it when the riot breaks out," Brock replies.

"I can't wait for the fun!" Zack says loudly, grinning. "Uncle Troy's signaling." He steps out of the alley. Chad and Brock follow. Troy is at the end of the street.

"Listen, Brock, I need to talk to you." Chad keeps his voice low. They are a dozen feet behind Zack, hopefully out of earshot.

"What's that?"

"I don't want the others to hear. It's about Ange."

Brock stops and looks at him. "What about Ange?"

"I saw her. She's with Antifa Latifa and . . ."

"What? Are you sure?"

"Yes. In front of the costume shop."

"Why the hell didn't you get her away from there?" Brock asks.

"I tried to. She wouldn't come."

"You telling me my sister's been kidnapped by Antifa?"

"Nothing I could do," Chad says.

"Why're you two standing around?" Troy shouts at them. "We got a mission to accomplish."

Chad follows Brock to the corner, where Troy and Zack await.

"What were you arguing about?" Troy asks.

"Nothing," Brock says.

"No? Good. We need to stick with the mission. Can't have anyone pussy-ing out."

"We're good," Brock says.

"Great. Follow me."

They step out of the side street. Ahead they can hear the hubbub of the crowd, a drone of chanting, and other noises outside the election offices and in the small park across the street. Keeping pace with the others, Chad's pulse quickens as the sounds get closer.

"Listen," Brock whispers to him when the others are six feet ahead. "We got to find her, make her get away before all fuck breaks loose. Even if we have to smack some skulls."

"But Troy wants us to stick with him," Chad says.

"I know. But she's my sister."

8

The police have the streets blocked off to vehicular traffic. Ange takes deep breaths as she follows the others through the outskirts, where people arrive from all directions, all headed to the same place. The mask makes her feel conspicuous rather than anonymous, but Ethan's hand squeezing hers is reassuring. Ethan has an eye mask with a beaked nose, showing less face than her own. They follow Jerry, Latifa, and Suzy into the thicker crowds.

With the signs and the chanting and the people in costumes, there is a festive atmosphere, though tinged with fear, excitement, and danger.

People from all walks of life are there. Families and groups and couples and the single loner, walking through the crowds and peering among faces. The unfamiliar faces. So many people gathered, some with loudspeakers, others banging on drums, even a small marching band at one spot, noises from every part of the park and the street.

Many have signs raised, printed ones and hand-made ones, some quite witty and others more profane. The noise from the crowd is deafening. One group chants "stop the steal" and another chants "count every vote," while amplified voices crackle over the din. A block away several vans await, packed with police. A half dozen men in identical camo and ammo belts, with frog masks and berets, march briskly, parting the people at the outskirts. Another group has matching hats and suits, and another wear Hawaiian shirts with MAGA caps, the uniform Ange has seen her brother and his friends wear. She searches among their faces, a few vaguely familiar, but neither her brother nor Chad is among them.

It's as if every oath keeper, three percenter, sovereign citizen, and militia member from hundreds of miles away has come down to counter the old hippies and angry grandmas and union people and dispossessed, and wild-eyed college kids a few years younger than her.

"Let's push forward," Latifa says. "I see people I know."

"You know everyone, girl," Jerry quips.

Ethan pulls Ange along, trailing the others. "You okay?" he asks.

"I think so. So many people here. I didn't know what to expect."

"Up there," he says. "The black block. Antifa." She follows his finger. Ten or twelve people in black, their faces completely covered with masks or scarves. "Probably good to keep away from them. In case fighting breaks out between them and . . ." He stops. "Where did the others go?"

"I don't think I've ever been among so many people," she says. She looks over at a group of four Antifa in black hoodies a dozen yards away. One turns towards her. The face is masked, a featureless mirror with just holes for the eyes, mouth, and nose. Another turns towards her too, same type of mask. She's about to turn away when the two figures begin to move towards her.

It's just her imagination, she thinks, a coincidence, since she can't see what they are looking at beneath those masks, but when Ethan pulls her forward a dozen steps, the two Antifa reroute their path to keep her in front of them as they push past other people.

"Ethan?"

"What is it?"

"I think those . . ." But that's silly. Why would Antifa want anything to do with her?

He glances over at the two men. His hand tightens on hers. "That mask. It's like the one from the store the Q-Anon dickhead took from me."

"Chad? But he's not Antifa."

The two masked men are seven feet away and coming directly towards her.

9

Brock burns with anger as he glances at the crowds. Anger at Antifa, anger at that college guy Ange brought to the house, anger at Ange. How could she be so stupid and gullible? Why didn't Chad get her away from the extremists before they brought her here?

He and Chad are several feet behind Troy and Zack, twisting their way through the crowds in the park across the street from the election offices. Zack has the messenger bag with the flash grenade.

"She has a pink mask," Chad says over the din. "One that goes over the eyes, like a raccoon."

"You see her?"

"Not yet."

"All we need is for that fucking idiot Zack to throw the flash grenade at Antifa Latifa and hit Ange."

"They said it wasn't dangerous," Chad says.

"Not as dangerous as a regular grenade, but if you're too near . . ."

"Brock, I think I spot her." Chad grabs his shoulder and Brock stops too.

"Where?" Brock turns to look. He spots her, recognizing the tee she wore earlier. Up ahead Troy and Zack continue to push through the crowd. "Let's go," Brock tells Chad.

"Shouldn't we tell Troy? He said to stick together."

"Not enough time. We get her to leave and then meet back with them. We can't lose her." Brock veers off, headomg towards Ange. Chad follows. She has her head turned towards them, and begins to move again. Brock recognizes the kid next to her, the same college boy who was at Dad's house, in a yellow mask similar to her pink one.

Brock pushes past more people. Ange is directly in front of him.

10

"Where the hell are the others?" Troy demands. "We must stick together."

"I think I see them." Zack points. Four or five Antifa in similar hoodies and masks, the real deal and not Brock or Chad. Zack isn't the sharpest tool in the box.

Troy scans the crowds. "This way. Stay with me." Moving through the crowd, he cringes at the people around him. Mindless zombies, with their similar signs and their meaningless chants. Old hippy zombies with drug-deadened brains, not realizing the sixties ended over fifty years ago, and younger zombies, crazy-eyed by leftist propaganda that has infiltrated every arm of media and the public education system, these social justice warriors, the openly queer trans who want to rub their amoral perversions in Christian faces, and so many others, the woke detritus of a sick society. Brainwashed zombies, all of them.

But things will change once his side wins the election. They'll bring back order with a vengeance. Through Schedule F Appointments, they'd eliminate corruption in the civil service, replace those who stood in the way with party loyalists who would do what was needed to stay in power. No more vulgarity, no more blasphemy, no more weakness and woke-ness. The morally corrupt will no longer stand in the way of the Great Awakening.

Troy spots two figures in hoodies and mirror masks. "Over there!" he tells Zack. "Follow me."

Why the hell did they wander off like that? Why did he think he could trust them? Zack might be an idiot, but at least Zack follows orders. But these two, at least he thought Brock had enough sense.

As he steps closer, it becomes clear. The two are engaging the enemy!

11

"Ange!"

"Brock? Why are you . . .? You're not Antifa."

"Why didn't you answer my texts?" Brock asks.

"Didn't feel like it."

"No time to explain. You got to leave."

"You can't tell me to leave!" Ange says.

"A bomb is going off!" Brock says.

"A what?"

"A bomb. Very soon. You need to get the hell out!"

"A bomb?" she gasps. "And why the Antifa get-up?"

"Jerry!" Ethan waves. Jerry with his camera appears from the crowd, followed by Latifa and Suzy. At the same time a pair of Antifa, in masks and hoodies similar to Brock's and Chad's, emerge from the crowd.

"Stop arguing with me!" Brock's voice is desperate. "You need to go!"

"Listen to your brother," Chad says. "A bomb's going off."

"Damn it, Brock! Chad!" Troy's voice is livid beneath the mask. "If you've been marked we have to abort mission."

"Doing the mission now, Uncle Troy?" Zack zips open the duffelbag.

"What do you mean a bomb?" Ethan sputters.

"Brock is right. You need to run, Ange. He's got a bomb!" Chad turns and points.

"What the hell are you doing?" Troy cocks his hand back and swings. The fist smacks into Chad's masked face and he flies into some elderly women with pro-choice signs.

"Where should I throw it, Uncle Troy?" Zack pulls out the device, a gray cylinder the size of a fire extinguisher.

"Abort mission, Zack! Abort mission!"

"Abortionists?" Zack asks, looking around. "Where?" He squints to read the pro-choice signs held by several old ladies. "Over there, Uncle Troy?"

Someone nearby screams. Ange and Ethan stare at the bomb in Zack's hand. Ethan lets go of her hand. Ange freezes in panic.

"Abort mission, Zack, damn it!"

"I see them, Uncle Tony!" Zack reaches for the firing pin.

Ethan leaps and hurls himself at Zack. They fly into bystanders. The flash bomb rolls away from them, the pin intact.

"Bomb!" Latifa yells. "Everyone back away!" The crowd begins to move back and spreads, like ripples from a rock dropped in water. Panic and confusion on faces. Zack shoves Ethan away, and twists around, looking for the bomb, at the same time reaching into the duffelbag.

Another bomb, Ange thinks. He has another bomb. "Ethan! Watch out!" she screams. While watching, she scrambles into her purse and pulls out a small canister of mace. Instead of backing away with the others, she dashes forward. Zack's hand flies clear of the duffel and he has a large revolver in it that he's about to aim at Ethan, who is ready to lunge at him again. Ange raises the mace. Zack swings the gun towards her. She releases the mace from the canister as she hurls towards him, the spray hits him square in the eyes.

Zack howls in agony and grabs for his eyes with his free hand as he waves the gun around. Ethan tackles him, throws him to the ground. Latifa and Suzy continue to get people to back away and Jerry catches it all on his video camera. The bomb sits by itself on the ground, scary even with the firing pin still intact. Chad and Brock help Ethan hold Zack down.

"Uncle Troy! Help!" Zack wails. "Where's Uncle Troy?"

12

Expecting at any moment to hear the blast over the din, Troy races through the crowd, knocking people out of the way with elbows and arms. Weak people, skinny or over-weight or too young or too old, useless people who want a bloated government to do everything for them, so many of them everywhere, a sea of enemies.

The crowd falls away, and before he can stop he hurls into the side of a large man in camo, pushing the man into others. He recognizes them, a local militia group. He starts to explain he is sorry.

"Scum!" The man swings at Troy. The others turn towards Troy. "Antifa!" someone yells.

"No!" Troy rips off his mask in hopes they'll recognize him, but too late. A truncheon smacks hard across his face. Stars flash in his head and he falls to the ground. When he opens his eyes, the militia has moved away. Several blurred faces are above him, medics and police.

"They caught the other one," says a gruff voice.

"I know this man." He recognizes the voice of Officer Mike McGinnis, his man on the police force. "I can vouch for him. He's no terrorist."

13

"You're a hero," Ange says to Ethan. "You stopped him from throwing that bomb."

"Me? No." Ethan shakes his head. "You're the hero. You stopped him, not me. You saved my life."

"It happened so fast. I didn't think about it."

They drink beers at a sports bar, the large television screens turned to cable news election coverage. The park at the election offices has mostly been cleared of supporters from both sides. The bomb never went off, the riot never happened, and the perpetrator identified as a right-wing extremist, two others have confessed to the bomb plot. Meanwhile, across the country things are worse, riots and assaults, a fist fight among poll watchers at one site, a central election office overtaken by an armed militia in another, and legislators in a couple of states demanding National Guard seize voting machines in urban areas.

"All this chaos. I just hope . . ." Ethan takes a swig of beer.

Ange glances at her phone wistfully. "Brock will probably get time."

In a far corner of the pub, several men in Hawaiian shirts watch a television tuned to a different news station. An Antifa terrorist named Zack Majors has been caught trying to bomb the election office, and Randy Know's image, from a cell phone, provides an eyewitness account. When the story ends, the men raise their beers in a toast.

"Good job, Randy."

Randy Know gleams proudly. "We'll get the truth out there. And when our guy wins, we'll end the lies. We'll get rid of the fake news." He looks at his phone. "And Troy has arrived."

At the other end of the pub, the front door opens and Troy enters. A dozen steps into the room, he pauses and walks over to a table. Ange and Ethan look up from their beers. Troy's gun beneath his shirt clanks against the side of the table.

"I know you. Brock's sister, aren't you?"

Ange nods.

Troy leans closer, voice low and smoldering. "Your brother and his friend Chad are fucking traitors."

"What was that about?" Ethan asks as Troy saunters toward his friends in the back.

"I think we should leave." On her feet, Ange grabs his hand. "We should leave now."

A Note from the author

This is a self-published novel. You can help make it a success:
* Tell friends about this book.
* Post reviews on amazon.com and goodreads.com
* Share this book on social media networks and blogs.
Thank you for reading books.
Rolf Semprebon

About Rolf Semprebon

For 15 years Rolf Semprebon (he/him) wrote scripts for a monthly radio theater show, The Ubu Hour, on KBOO Community Radio, and has also published music reviews in several publications. The Oregon Writers Colony awarded him honorable mention in their 2019 Fiction First Chapter Contest. He's also had short stories published in Aether Avenue Press and Unnamed Journal in 2024 and in Northwest Independent Writers Association anthology Journey in 2025. Rolf grew up in New Hampshire, graduated from Oberlin College, and lives in Portland Oregon with his cat.